Granite Lake Wolves

Wolf Signs

Wolf Flight

Wolf Games

Wolf Tracks

Wolf Line

Wolf Nip

Takhini Wolves

Black Gold

Silver Mine

Diamond Dust

Moon Shine

Takhini Shifters

Copper King

Laird Wolf

A Lady's Heart

Wild Prince

A full list of Vivian's print titles is available on her website

www.vivianarend.com

PRAISE FOR VIVIAN AREND

"Vivian Arend does a wonderful job of building the atmosphere and the other characters in this story so that readers will be sucked into the world and looking forward to the rest of the books in the series."
~ *Library Journal*

"Steamy and sweet complete with a whole host of colourful side characters and enough sub-plots to get your teeth into. A fab read!"
~ *Scorching Book Reviews*

"There's a real chemistry between the characters, laced with humor and snappy dialogue and no shortage of steamy sex scenes to keep things lively. The result is an entertaining, spicy romance."
~ *Publishers Weekly*

Silver Mine is an outstanding story. The author creates a world that invites readers for the ride of their lives."
~ *Coffee Time Romance Reviews*

Arend offers constant action and thrills, and her characters are so captivating and nuanced that readers will have a hard time guessing who the villains really are.
~ *RT Book Reviews*

WOLF LINE

NORTHERN LIGHTS EDITION

VIVIAN AREND

This is a work of fiction. Names, characters, places, and incidents either are the product of the author's imagination or are used fictitiously, and any resemblance to any persons, living or dead, business establishments, events, or locales is entirely coincidental.

For everyone who's told me the wolfies make them smile. For Sarah, Natasha, Nicole, Barbara, and too many more to name. Thanks for giving me a reason to keep coming back to play in the Granite Lake world.

1
———

The alternating colours of cream and coffee revolved like hypnotic artwork as a finger of steam rose from the surface of his drink. Jared Gilliland took a long sip and waited for the caffeine to soak through his system and kick his brain awake.

There was nothing better than enjoying an invigorating cup of java while relaxing on the premier harbour-view patio in all of Haines. He turned his face toward the early July sunshine, and contentment rolled over him.

Okay, the fact he'd had a wickedly pleasurable night the previous evening with a sweet young thing also had something to do with the lazy satisfaction in his limbs.

Life was good. A trifle frustrating at times, perhaps, but on the whole, damn good.

"If I didn't know better, I'd think you'd been up to something, just from your expression."

Jared popped upright from his sprawl to discover his Beta closing in on the table. The massive man carried a tray covered with mugs. Behind him trailed a convoy of the Granite Lake wolves. Jared jumped to his feet and pulled a chair out of Erik's way. "Who, me? Up to something? You're just saying that because nine times out of ten, it's true."

Erik chuckled as he lowered his burden to the table. "I like that about you. Honest enough to admit your faults."

"Well, now, I didn't say it was a fault—creativity is one of my better qualities." He dipped his head politely to Keil and Robyn, the pack Alphas, before glancing at the diminishing space around his table. "Umm, did you want me to leave?"

"Of course not." Keil rested his hand on Robyn's shoulder to hold her back for a second. "I thought you'd picked the best table in the place especially so we'd join you. You don't mind, do you?"

Hot damn, no. This might not be as restful a morning as Jared had planned, but getting to spend time with the bigwigs of the pack was worth giving up a little R and R. "Happy to be of service. I've been fighting people off left and right to save this spot."

Chairs settled in place, cups and goodies were passed out, and then there were seven. Jared might have felt more anxious if all of them weren't so well known to him. From Keil and Robyn to Tad and Missy, who acted as Omegas for the pack, Jared had watched with admiration over the past two and a half years as they'd worked from within the Alaskan wolf pack to make it stronger than before.

Erik and his mate Maggie—he'd spent time with them on the trail during the wolf equivalent of the Amazing Race. It was tough to be intimidated by someone he'd crawled over rocks and splashed through creeks with.

"What's the word on the renovations?" Keil tapped the table in front of Maggie. "And please tell me you're not still trying to get the Teslin brothers to finish the plumbing for the new kitchen."

"Hey, they have the skills. They've been a little distracted over the past couple weeks." She shook her head and pointed at Erik. "It's his fault."

"Mine?"

"Yours. You gave approval for the contractor from the cruise ship to use the hall in the pack house for interviews. I can't blame the guys for getting distracted when there's been a constant stream of good-looking female wolves parading through the—"

Jared spoke without thinking. "Good-looking wolves?"

A sharp burst of laughter surrounded him, and he might have flushed for a moment. His reputation, well deserved, preceded him. He smiled sheepishly and grabbed a sip of his coffee. Lowering his cup revealed Robyn's bright grin directly across from him.

They'd arranged themselves without thinking to make it easy for her to see their faces. Her skills in lip reading hadn't changed when she became a full wolf, but somehow her deafness had become even less of an obstacle. She had an uncanny knack of analyzing people that allowed her to fit in easily with the hearing community. Of course, her willingness to slap down any out-of-line wolf might also explain why the pack remained on their best behavior around her.

Robyn spoke in sign language to her mate, and Keil laughed even harder. "I agree."

Jared pressed closer. "What? I didn't catch that."

Keil tilted his cup toward Jared. "She was wondering why any of us are surprised to find your attention was caught by the idea of good-looking wolves. You've gone through the most amazing collection of females of anyone I've ever met. Before I met Robyn, I used to have a fair number..."

He trailed off as she crossed her arms, her expression changing subtly. Jared stifled his snort of amusement.

"...used to have all kinds of trouble finding a good woman to spend time with." Keil folded his hands in front of him, resting his hamlike fists on the table. He smiled innocently at Robyn like a four-year-old, and not one of the scariest dudes in the entire state of Alaska, in human or wolf form. "There simply wasn't anyone who could measure up to my high standards. I lived a sad and lonely life until you came into my world."

She smiled and patted his cheek.

Erik shook his head. "We'll all ignore the fact you just lied through your teeth."

Maggie nodded in agreement, her blonde curls bouncing. "That would be less complicated, wouldn't it?"

The teasing carried on for a while, and Jared basked in a different kind of warmth than he'd been enjoying at the start of his coffee break.

Pack was family, and his had turned into one of the best around. Granite Lake had changed for the better over the past couple years. The group of shifters surrounding him was powerful enough to keep even unruly wolves in line, but they did it in a totally personable and fun way. There were new members coming to Haines all the time now wanting to join. It wasn't just a remote place to live anymore. The harbourside Alaskan town had so much to offer to the new breed of adventurer moving north.

Not that he longed for adventure. Nope. The quiet life was more than enough of an exploit for him. He supposed. The yearning inside for something more could be shoved aside for a while longer.

Someone poked him in the arm. "You found a job for the summer yet?"

Jared scrambled mentally, pulling himself from his doldrums. One of the unwritten pack rules was work or they'd find work for you. He'd kept his actual business connections on the sly for so long, everyone thought the principle still applied to him. "Of course."

Tad waited.

"Well, strictly speaking, it's not a *job* job, but I promised to help at the Heritage Village while the cruise ships are in port. You know, dressing up and—"

"Seducing the visitors? Oh, Jared, when are you going to grow up and get going with your life?" Maggie shook her head, but she was smiling too hard to actually be upset.

Busted. That was a sweet side bonus. "Hey, positive tourism is a good thing for Haines. I figure the happier people are when they leave our fair shores, the better chance they'll return."

"And the casual hookups aren't something you mind, right?" All the men at the table stared at Maggie in undisguised shock. She rolled her eyes. "Damn sex junkies, all you male wolves. Okay, let me rephrase that. Aren't you looking for something more than casual sex at some point?"

Jared waited a full five seconds out of respect before blurting, "No. Never. Like not ever."

Six heads swiveled his direction, and this time even the guys seemed to be laughing at him and not with him.

"You're going to be such a goner when you meet your mate." Tad brushed his fingers through the pale curls at the base of Missy's neck. Jared considered making a smart-ass comment, but thought better of it. Tad could use his freaky Omega spidey-senses and find out exactly how and why Jared didn't expect to ever find his mate. And then there would be all kinds of questions and an inquisition...

From the pointed look he got from Missy, it might be too late.

Damn mystical wolf voodoo—keeping secrets from this group took more energy than hiding catnip from a bunch of cougar shifters.

Luckily, the Omegas were polite enough to not start scanning pack members without a reason like some out-of-control wolf TSA. She wouldn't say anything in front of the whole pack, if she had caught his secret.

And secrets he had.

He adjusted his chair, hoping to fade into the background. Erik winked slyly then changed the topic. Jared made a mental note to buy a six-pack of the dude's favourite brew and slip it onto his porch. Yeah, the Beta was one of the golden boys of the pack.

Actually, they were all fabulous. He had no issues with any of the leadership. Life was grand, other than his itchy feet and his one little issue, and that was something no one could help him with, so it was less of an *issue* and more of a *thing*. Things could be ignored.

Conversation picked up again, and he relaxed, taking the time to examine the faces around him as they visited. He checked out the mix of humans and shifters crowded into the little coffee shop and the second-story balcony seating on this glorious July morning. Down on the street, two heftily built fishermen moved northward, coming from the harbour.

Why did they look familiar? He didn't think they were shifters, and he didn't usually hang out at the docks. Jared leaned forward and stared harder. They turned to look in his direction, and as he met their eyes, their expressions twisted from rather mindless to furious.

Jared glanced behind him. Nope. No one there the boys could be pissed at. Had Erik or Keil done something?

"Umm, anyone been annoying the locals lately? The pack got any unpaid bills at the fishmongers?"

Erik frowned. "What?"

"Someone down there is very interested in someone up here." Jared pointed, and the entire table turned toward the street.

Of course, that was the moment Jared figured out exactly why the men's features were familiar. The adrenaline that flashed through his veins was stronger than the kickback jolt from a dozen triple espressos—body instantly on edge, heart pounding. He snuck his chair back, planted one hand on the railing behind him, and threw himself over.

"Are you sure everything is in place?"

Keri crossed her arms and leaned on the wall outside the cruise ship's command room. "At some point you have to get over this irritating urge to micromanage every single step of the journey. Tessa, everything is going to be okay. The cruise is fully booked. All the passengers have cleared the security check. Willis got the final staff we need in place— you can relax."

Her best friend nodded, even as she rapidly puffed air. Keri looked around helplessly for a paper bag to shove over Tessa's head. Hyperventilation wasn't pretty to watch.

Tessa held up her arms and shook her hands as if she were greeting aliens. "It's just, this has to be perfect."

"Oh great, like no pressure on any of us. Even your brother

didn't run the ship with an impeccable record. Give yourself a break." This wasn't only *first day on the job* nerves, this was *living up to being the little sister* nerves. "The cruise leaves in a couple hours. Everyone will have an awesome time, reports will go out on all the tourist sites that Arctic Wolf Cruise Lines still runs the best getaway-slash-northern-experience ever. The shifter news network will rave about how sweet it is to have an exclusive cruise where going furry isn't frowned upon."

"But what if something goes wrong?" Tessa's eyes widened. "What if the Fedoras don't have a good time? Keri, why did they have to choose my maiden voyage to take a trip? Having royalty on board makes it worse. I keep thinking I should wear a corset and full-length skirt, and carry a fan when I greet them."

Keri eyed Tessa's pale face. "You going to swoon? Because I can get you some smelling salts, but I'm not sure what they would do to your metabolism. Aren't cats allergic?"

"Shut up." Tessa grimaced her way into a smile. "I get it. I'll stop having kittens. I just...I just want to do well."

"I know you do." Keri grabbed Tessa by the elbow and pulled her toward the pilothouse. "Your family has operated this cruise line for years. It's your turn to take up the torch, *yada, yada, yada.*"

Tessa tucked her arm through Keri's, and they walked side-by-side, the position comfortable and easy. Her friend's tension slowly faded as they strode the halls talking about not much of anything. Keri smiled. If there was one thing she'd learned living next door to cat shifters for years, felines needed to move.

"For my first recommendation as troubleshooter, I suggest you get your rebounder out. Pop it in the corner of your office. Actually, screw that. Put it behind your desk and use it instead of a chair."

Tessa laughed. "I'm going to look oh-so-professional bouncing up and down as I talk to the crew."

"Better than bouncing off the walls." Keri squeezed her friend's arm. "I know we kid around a lot, but I do think you're going to rock this. You've got the skills. So what if Big Brother Golden Boy would do some things differently? Be yourself, use those freaky managerial skills you got at that fancy-schmancy school, and everything will work out fine."

They pulled to a stop outside Tessa's office door. Tessa whirled on her. "I'm glad you're here. You're the best friend ever."

All light vanished as Keri was buried in an enormous hug, her face jammed into Tessa's armpit, her ribs groaning in protest.

"Hey there, Tigger, lighten up on the full-body attacks."

The words squeaked out like a ducky on its final float in the tub. Tessa released her and Keri sucked for air, maintaining her smile even as she gasped for breath.

The cougar shifter who was her best friend in the world, and as near to a sister as anyone could be, bounced in a circle around her. "I mean it, Keri. Thanks for lending a hand. It's not everyone who would give up their holiday to work."

"Hey, I'm on a cruise ship. Bonbons and swimming pools. Exactly how much exertion is this going to take?" Keri ducked Tessa's halfhearted swing. "Kidding, kidding—but come on, I'm nothing but a glorified gofer. It's not as if I'm cooking for five hundred."

"That would be scariness of epic proportions." Tessa gave an exaggerated shudder and clutched her stomach.

Keri snorted. "Right. You can't cook either."

"I'm surprised we didn't starve during college."

"Ahh, the wonders of microwave dinners and pizza delivery." Keri gave her friend a light punch in the shoulder. "But we survived that, you'll make it through this. More than survive—you're gonna do awesome."

"Thanks." Tessa let out a deep breath before giving her a wink. "Thanks for reminding me I can do it."

They fist-bumped, then Tessa slipped into her office and Keri headed down the hall to escape onto deck.

She took it all in—the beautiful blue sky, the undulating waves of the ocean. The scent of the sea and a faint hint of fried food from the restaurants of the town filled her nostrils. She leaned on the railing and smiled.

It *was* a holiday. Tessa might be in the middle of panic mode, but those were normal first-time-out nerves. The shifter-only cruises had operated without a hitch for years, and with Tessa at the helm, nothing would change except maybe to get better. Like the rest of her family—the clan that had provided Keri's second home for the past ten years —the girl had a flair for making others happy.

Volunteering as a troubleshooter wasn't going to be a huge task at all. It was more a favour to ease Tessa's concerns.

No, Keri planned on using what should be ample spare time this trip to plan out her future. She had an art degree from the community college, ink permanently staining her fingers, and a backpack full of charcoal pencils and art pads. But drawing pictures in the farmer's market wouldn't pay the bills forever. She sent another set of good wishes her parents' direction for being patient with a rebellious hothead and giving her a place to bloom.

Now if she could only figure out what she wanted to be when she grew up.

A gust of wind tossed her long hair into her eyes, and Keri regretted her decision to leave it down. At sea she'd have to drag it back into a ponytail. She twisted the strands out of her way and dug in her pocket for an elastic.

Loud shouts drew her attention to the harbour. Three people raced through the streets, the one in front narrowly ahead. He leapt over a stack of boxes before shoving them behind him into the path of his pursuers. The first man turned the corner, out of sight for a moment, as the two behind forced the crates out of the way, their curses painting the air blue.

Keri walked along the railing, trying to locate the cause of the commotion. Was he a thief, perhaps? Someone late on their mooring payments? By the time she'd reached the prow of the boat, the two pursuers were visible in greater detail. Big clumpy fishermen boots graced their feet, and they were covered in shiny rain gear from head to toe. The sheer awkwardness of running in those outfits made her legs ache in sympathy.

Out on the main street, a lone figure dashed back into view, head down, legs pumping. He was poetry in motion as he leapt over ropes and around barrels, climbing over people and shipping supplies as if taking a casual stroll down the beach.

Only, when he changed direction, raced up the ramp and disappeared into the depths of the *Arctic Wolf*'s hold, the fun and games were over.

"Oh, no you don't." Keri turned to the nearest stairwell and sprinted downward.

Troubleshooter? This was trouble shouting loud and clear, and no way was someone sneaking aboard the ship unapproved. Not on her watch. Especially someone who might or might not have the fishermen's mafia on his heels.

She burst into the crew common area and glanced around. A short line of people waited before a folding table, the two pursers behind it handing out keys and information sheets.

"Something wrong?" The chief supervisor, Chad, smiled her way enticingly, and yeah, they'd been flirting earlier, but...timing, dude. Being a family friend didn't mean *any time, any place.*

"Did you see an unauthorized entry? There was a disturbance down on the docks."

"No one new boarded except the last-minute crew we contracted locally. And this is almost the last of them." Chad stood and eyed the line. "There's one missing. A Mark Weaver. He's not here yet—"

"Here I am. Sorry. Tiny mistake—alarm didn't go off. Got here as quick as possible."

The late arrival was dark haired, the strands long enough to lie tousled around his shoulders like some bad-boy rock star on tour. *Mmm,* she liked bad boys. His leather jacket hung open, his chest moving rapidly, and Keri hesitated.

Chest heaving? Slightly panting—as if he'd been running? "Did someone escort you to the ship, Mr. Weaver?"

His eyes widened, then his grin flashed and her belly warmed. Damn, that face of his should be labeled a dangerous weapon. "No, but I sure could use an escort to my room."

"You'll get your sleeping assignment in a minute," Chad cut in. "First, sign here."

Keri shook herself, stepping back in self-defense.

Mark winked her direction then leaned over the table to

add a swirl of chaos to the bottom of the page. "There you go, love."

Chad choked for a second before handing over a key. "Your room is on the port side, toward mid ship. You can get extra linens and supplies from the hall storage, and your first shift starts at eleven hundred hours. Report back here and you'll find your team leader. They'll get you fitted up and give you any last-minute instructions."

Mark tilted an imaginary hat at Keri, ignoring Chad completely. "You going to be around? Help me find my sea legs, that kind of thing?"

Keri continued to retreat until her back hit the wall. "I think we'll end this conversation now, Mr. Weaver. Find your quarters."

His dark eyes sparkled for a second before he dropped his gaze, stroking his way down her body. She should have felt insulted. She should've turned and demanded he treat her with more respect. The words wouldn't come, mainly because what she really wanted was to strip right there and ride him like a Harley. Feel his power rumbling between her thighs and—

Sweat broke out on her brow, cooling instantly in the air-conditioned room. Mark was out the door before she figured out how to respond further. Keri avoided the blatant question in Chad's eyes and raced away, slamming through the door that led the opposite direction from where her mystery man had gone. All thoughts of why he'd been chased aboard were lost in the disastrous new revelation that had overtaken her.

This was not good. This was *so* not good. The situation had gone from troublesome to tortuous in less time than it took for the average wolf pack to consume a prime-rib dinner.

Keri stopped to lean her forehead on the nearest wall. She hit with more force than intended, which was moderately excruciating but somehow appropriate.

In fact, she repeated the move. A couple of times.

Bang. Bang.

The resulting pain made her screw up her face. *Bang.* She was supposed to be there for her friend and act as a troubleshooter. *Bang.* Not be the one to cause chaos right under Tessa's nose. *Bang.* Not discovering her mate in the midst of the hired help.

Her mate. *Oh my word, was it really him?*

She flipped around and pressed her shoulders to the wall, letting her head fall back. Instantly drooling over some strange guy wasn't the problem—shifters were cool about sex, and if she wanted to go knock boots with someone, no one would even blink.

But what her body was doing right now? This was an out-of-the-blue, off-the-charts, do-it-now and do-it-hard attraction. In any shifter's handbook, she was sure she'd find her symptoms listed as classic *he's the one,* accompanied by flashing neon warning lights.

Now the question was, what the heck did she do?

2

———

*J*ared sprawled across the single bed that occupied three-quarters of the available space in his tiny crew cabin. Ever since his fight-or-flight response had kicked in back at the coffee shop and shot him full of adrenaline, he'd been vibrating. Only now had his heart rate dropped to anything approaching normal.

He sat up and dragged a hand through his hair. Well, that had been exciting. His lover over the previous few nights had insisted she was good with some casual fun. The family photo he'd spotted on the wall, the one with her being guarded carefully by her older brothers—his chasers of the fisherman variety—should have reminded him otherwise. Even if she was fine with bed-rocking, mind-blowing, no-strings-attached sex, her big brothers had other ideas about what their little sis should be doing. They had warned him off a long time ago.

His reputation truly had been well earned.

Bursting in on the cruise-ship staff gathering put a temporary kink in his plans to simply hide out for a few minutes until the bruiser boys left the area. He'd been ready

15

to cut and return to Haines, peeking down the corridor he'd run up, when the stiff from the sign-in table, that Chad somebody, had taken it upon himself to provide a door-to-door escort to his staff quarters.

In spite of the hole he was in, Jared had to laugh.

Stepping forward and claiming to be Mark—sheer impulse on his part. The guy was one of the Granite Lake pack, and pulling practical jokes on each other came with the territory.

This prank was the best so far, especially since he'd seen Mark tossing back a few too many last night. Jared bet his friend was somewhere off in Haines, face down, drooling and snoring, happily unaware he was late for his assignment.

Jared wondered what the pack would think up for work for the dude. Hopefully something physically dirty and nasty. Not that he was vindictive or anything, but the last time they'd officially faced off, Mark had stiffed him with the bill for an entire night's food and drink.

Jared headed for the door. Time for the fun and games to be over. Maybe he'd even be nice and phone Mark once he got down on the docks. Give the guy a wake-up call and all that. He poked his head out the door and pulled up short.

Chad glanced over from where he stood chatting with a couple girls in housekeeping uniforms—neither of whom Jared recognized.

"Need something?" Suspicion tinged Chad's voice.

Shit. "Nope. Just curious. Thought I heard a large donkey in the hallway. No worries..."

He ducked back into his room and closed the door on the sound of feminine laughter and Chad's cussing.

Oh yeah, it was a good thing this was a temporary gig. Chad was far too easy to tease.

Jared made his way over to the tiny window and cupped his hands around his eyes to block the room light. He peered out, fascinated to see the people boarding the ship. Bags and boxes were being rolled up a gangplank, and all over the dock there was excitement and energy. Dynamic, thrilling.

A huge yawn broke free and he stretched lazily. Well, that was enough of that. He was more than ready to head home and crash for another few hours. Some time this afternoon he would show up at the Heritage Village. Maybe do a little shopping first...

When are you going to grow up?

Maggie's tease from the coffee shop echoed in his head. He felt a little guilty that people he admired had been completely taken in by his deception. All the more honest responses he could have given her blurred together into a confusing morass, compounded by this temporary excursion back into the world of the privileged.

It wasn't his first time on a cruise ship, and the percolating memories were both attractive and disturbing. Frustration made him revert to his usual coping strategy, which was to ignore the issue.

He snuck another peek out the door, delighted to find the hall empty. Jared whistled softly, making his way forward and glancing down hallways to figure his way out of the bowels of the ship.

A quick peek at his watch. Ten a.m. Lots of time. He could even get in a nap and game of pool before heading over to do some volunteer work. He took a set of stairs upward, weaving through increasing crowds as shifters in holiday garb filled the hallways.

Yup, this had been an interesting diversion, but it was time to get back to the real world. He had chosen a path years ago that meant avoiding all contact with cruise lines and upscale entertainments. A simple lifestyle, ordinary people—that was his destiny.

Mingling with the rich and famous was for other wolves, not him.

~

KERI SPLASHED cold water on her face, but the shock wasn't enough. Screw it. She twisted the taps in her sink on full then shoved her entire head under the faucet, icy water soaking her hair and spraying over her neck.

Lips sealed shut, she held her breath and stayed under as long as she could, hoping the frigid blast would wash away some of her frustration. But by the time she'd dragged herself out and wrapped a towel around her head, she was no better off than before. If anything, the wild itch under her skin had increased.

Maybe she could avoid him for the ten-day duration of the cruise. Then she'd jump him. That would work.

Mark Weaver. She wrinkled her nose. Not much to go on from a name. Curiosity struck. There had been a whole sheet of information compiled on each of the staff. Chad had the files. That was the first way to discover what she could about Mark—strictly so she could stay away from him, of course.

Not that she wasn't interested in getting to know her mate eventually, but until this cruise was over, she didn't have time to be rolling in the hallways with him.

A flash of heat roared up one side of her and down the other at the thought, and she wrapped both arms around her chest tightly to stop from getting naked and dealing with the ache herself.

She stood forlornly in the middle of her bathroom, a slow *drip, drip, drip* hitting the floor from her hair, wetness oozing through her clothing, making the fabric stick to her skin. In spite of the frigid water, her libido was still set to maximum. Her breasts ached, her sex felt empty and her heart pounded out a rumba-tango-fandango. Yeah, this wasn't good. If she didn't figure out a solution quick, she'd be tracking Mark down and humping him no matter where she found him.

She stripped off her wet things, ignoring the desire to linger over her extremely sensitive skin. A fresh pair of jeans, a clean T-shirt—it wasn't fancy but she was neither crew nor passenger. She could wear whatever she wanted. A pair of runners on her feet and she was off.

The carpet underfoot on the exclusive cabin level was thick enough to sink into on every step. Getting spoiled by being the friend of the organizer? She'd take it. Her cabin was way bigger than the crew hovels. She and Mark could totally use the king-sized bed in her cabin to—

No, not going there. She needed to turn off the GPS that seemed to have focused very firmly on *sex* and *Mark* and *mate*.

"If it isn't the most beautiful wolf on the boat."

Keri pulled to a stop and glanced behind her.

A dark chuckle stroked her ears. *Oh damn.* Chad.

"You, darling. I'm talking about you. What made you disappear earlier? I had hoped to talk you into checking out my cabin." He stepped into her personal space, his solid chest mere inches away from her.

Damn. Damn, damn, *poop*.

This wasn't unexpected at all. They'd been eyeing each

other for years. Chad had been best friends with Tessa's big brother all through high school, which meant Keri had seen him plenty. Now that they were in the same place at the same time, both supposedly free agents, becoming lovers would have been a pretty natural progression.

The big wolf smelt good. All those bulging muscles hovering within stroking reach were firm and tasty and... nothing. Her libido didn't register anything anymore. Not since she'd gotten a whiff of Mark.

"Hi, Chad."

She pressed harder against the wall, attempting to open up room between them.

He planted a palm beside her head and leaned in closer, breathing deeply. "Hi, Chad? That's all I get? This morning during the general staff meeting I could have sworn you said something to the effect of 'please rip off my panties with your teeth and lick me until I scream'."

Her cheeks heated. "I didn't say that."

"Not in words," he acknowledged, "but I know a *hey, you wanna fuck?* look when I see one."

Oh, brother. Yes, this morning she might have been guilty of sending out that vibe, but now she was pretty sure her signals were screaming a different message. "Do you also know the key components of a *warning, you're about to lose your nuts* look?"

He frowned then glanced upward. Wiggled his nose for a second, then shrugged. "Nope, I'm pretty sure I've never seen that one in my life."

"Chad, may I speak with you?" a bright feminine voice interrupted.

Keri breathed a sigh of relief as he turned toward the head of the housekeeping department. Good, he'd be distracted enough she could just...slip...

His other hand landed on the wall to her right, effectively blocking her escape route. "Is it an emergency, Eden?"

The dark-haired woman shook her head. "No, but—"

"Send me an email. We can discuss it during the staff meeting this afternoon."

"But—"

"Later, Eden." He dismissed her without a second glance.

Eden left, her expression unreadable. Keri felt strangely trapped. Well, more trapped than having Chad loom over her and basically pin her to the wall with his proximity. She didn't want to come between the man and his job.

Come to think of it, she didn't want to come between him and *anything*.

Keri planted both palms on his chest, preparing to shove him away when he caught her off guard and covered her mouth with his.

She was having an out-of-body experience. Watching from a foot or two over the hall as their lips meshed. He ground against her, their hips damn close to merging through osmosis.

He was buff and tan and surfer-dude gorgeous. Until an hour ago she'd been completely on board with having him in her bed every night, all cruise long.

Now? The loudest thing running through her brain was *gag*. The only sections of her mental synapses fully engaged were curiously pondering what Mark was doing. And then there was the question of whether the first time they did it, would they even make it to a bed? *Hmmm*. If this was Mark right now across from her, she'd grab his hips and—

"Ahem."

Light appeared as they were interrupted for a second

time. Chad retreated a couple inches to stare to their left at
—*oh damn*—it was Mark.

"Sorry, didn't mean to interrupt, but if you don't mind?"
He brushed a hand through his dark hair, leaving it in
unruly perfection.

Time stood still.

...because that was all he did.

Keri choked out a protest. "But...you...I'm...we're..."

Both men stared at her in confusion.

*Great job, idiot. Way to prove English is your mother
tongue.*

Chad glared at Mark. "You're not supposed to be on this
deck. It's off limits to maintenance crew."

Mark paused, then lifted a finger and shook it once.
"Yes. Right. Except I got lost. I was trying for the outside
deck. Just wanted a breath of fresh air before getting down
to work."

He eyed Keri, his predatory, mesmerizing, hungry gaze
returning. It was all she needed in the way of visual
foreplay. She sighed lustily, squeezing her legs together to
fight the flood of desire about to float her away. One hand
rose involuntarily in his direction.

He took her fingers and squeezed them.

She waited for him to haul them together. To drag her
from Chad's side. To toss her to the floor and mark her right
then and there. She felt it so strongly—the urge to mate.
The *need* to mate.

It was as if she'd been holding her breath, swimming
underwater for years, and only now moving toward the
surface. Urgency drove her. About to break the surface,
about to pull in life-giving air...

She lifted her chin. Tilted her head and offered her
lips.

"Nice to meet you again. Later." He dropped her hand and passed on by.

He might as well have planted a hand on her head and dunked her. She gasped, breathed wrong and inhaled spit. Hard coughing racked her.

"Hey, it's okay." Chad patted her back lightly, confusion blurring his features as she fought her way upright, watching Mark disappear down the hall.

He'd walked away.

He'd...walked away? *What the heck?*

"I don't understand." Her body ached, and her brain had gone numb.

"Ah, he's just one of the hired help. You won't have to see him again."

Chad cupped her face and pressed in again. Keri's skin crawled, goose bumps the side of Greenland rising. Not a good reaction.

He brushed his cheek against hers and purred. "Mmm, I can smell you."

What? Her mind was so muddled she had no idea what that meant for a moment. An idea hit, and she tilted her nose toward her armpit and sniffed.

Nope. That wasn't it.

A faint flicker of comprehension banged on the door blocking her thought processes. Her mate had walked past her down the hallway, ignoring the fact she was in another man's arms—again she squirmed inside with an *ick, ick, ick* —and left her?

Was Mark stark raving mad?

Chad groped her again, and her temper flew up faster than she could control. She shoved him violently enough he bounced off the far wall.

"Whoa, okay. So, in spite of your body saying you're

interested, you're going to play hard to get?" Chad nodded and stroked his chin thoughtfully. "Is this like a game?"

"That's not it. I'm not..." Keri paused.

Wait. Wait. No instant reactions to Chad.

She needed a coping strategy. She had to think this through. Her mate had some obvious issues. Maybe he was worried about his position. Maybe her...

It was as if a light bulb went off overhead. Inspiration rocked her. Actually, she was grabbing at straws to explain his non-reaction to her, but this was at least possible.

Maybe Mark didn't want her to get in trouble with the boss. Probably figured her job was on the line and breaking up with the chief supervisor wouldn't make him very happy.

What a sweetie. She blinked hard, her heart thumping as she sent all kinds of loving thoughts Mark's direction. A little wave of happiness bubbled inside. Her mate was a wonderful and insightful man.

Maybe. Hopefully.

She turned to Chad. "It's just that we're about to get under way. We'll talk about this later, okay? Bye then."

Sprinting down the hall would be undignified, so she maintained control and only walked fast. Really fast. She wasn't chasing Mark. Only wanted one more glimpse, that's all. Maybe shoot a few more good vibes his direction. The door to the deck swung open smoothly and she blasted out.

He stood not ten feet in front of her, head cocked to the right as he stared down at the dock from their upper-deck level. She froze, caught completely in the open. One tiny step at a time she inched toward the safety of the overhang where she could...

Not good. The broad measure of his back turned toward her. In a second they'd be face to face.

All confidence fled and her feet turned on high. She felt like the roadrunner cartoon, legs rotating in blurred circles. Skipping over the metal decking as she scurried to get out of sight.

She scrambled around the corner and ducked through an open door into an equipment room. Piles of shuffleboard and other deck games lay arranged on shelves and organized in neat totes. She eyed the open door with trepidation, holding her breath. When he walked past without spotting her, Keri gasped in relief.

One quick lunge was enough to grab the door and swing it shut, locking herself in the semi-darkness of the pristine chamber, the only light sneaking in from two small windows on the far wall. She hopped up on the largest storage container in the corner and collapsed. Okay, this was not going the way she'd planned.

"Brilliant, Smith. Simply brilliant. Get yourself out of this one."

She might have managed to avoid bumping into him, but the whole matter of how to cope with having her mate on board was still open.

Think. Think.

The only response was a heavy throb between her legs, and Keri cursed. Fine. It seemed there would be no thinking until she dealt with this outlandish need burning through her veins. She tugged at her T-shirt before giving in. The fabric came off one direction, her bra the other. Folding her palms over her breasts and squeezing let her deal with a bit of the urgency.

It wasn't enough. There was no way she could go back out there and do any kind of positive work without first letting off a little steam. She unzipped and slid her fingers into her pants.

~

THE BRUNETTE he'd just passed in the hall? Man, sometimes life sucked. She appeared to be just his type— feminine yet slightly on the naughty side. When they'd caught a glimpse of each other in the crew quarters earlier, he'd thought she'd checked him over with interest as well.

But Jared didn't poach. Love the ladies, love them thoroughly, but even within the sexually open shifter community there were rules. Keeping balls and body together was an important item on his to-do list, so in spite of her flushed skin and wild-eyed interest, he had walked away, escaping onto the deck.

And found himself at a dead end, any stairs headed toward the dock inaccessible from where he stood. Unless he wanted to leap over another railing—and thanks, no thanks, once a day doing *that* was his quota—he needed to find a new way down. Time was a-wasting.

Pacing the deck brought him to another dead end, and he growled in frustration. There wasn't a soul around— somehow he must have gotten into an area that was closed right now. He doubled back with the intention of retracing his steps through the hall. There had to be a way out of the maze. Jared glanced to the left and froze in his tracks as a very fine pair of breasts bounced at him.

He blinked.

They bounced again, and Jared moved closer to the window set into the metal wall and snapped his jaw shut. Suddenly leaving the ship wasn't nearly as important as it had been a few seconds ago. He tucked himself farther around the corner, making sure to maintain a clear view through the tiny window.

His mystery woman had stripped to the waist, leaning

back as if she were a smorgasbord offering. When her hand slipped out of sight under the edge of her open jeans, he slapped his own hand over his groin in self-defense.

If he hadn't just seen her lip-locked with another guy, he'd be in there. Helping her find a more comfortable position, preferably on his tongue.

A stiff breeze kicked up, and he twisted away from it, being careful he didn't obey his first instinct which was to press his face full against the glass like some panting dog to get a better view. Instead, he snuck to the next window where he was tucked around the corner and hidden from sight. Maybe he hadn't seen a soul for the past ten minutes, but no need to take a chance.

His wolf rumbled, but he beat the beast down. Poor thing was always getting at him for one reason or another. While that side of his nature was constantly there, didn't mean he had to act like an animal.

A low moan carried through the wall, and the fact they were both shifters made him very happy. He felt comfortable watching, confident she wouldn't really mind. On the whole, sex was cool. But not cheating—that was completely ix-nay, out of bounds.

Watching wasn't cheating. It was just...admiring and taking notes. In case he did get a chance with her in the future. That's all.

Luckily he was a genius at rationalization.

She slid lower on the platform, opening up more room in her pants. He watched the fabric move against her hand, the noises she made driving him crazy. A groaner. *Hmmm.* Bet he could make her scream. He loved women who were noisy in bed.

One rapid glance ensured there was no one around, so Jared pulled out his cock. Tucked behind a large pillar, he was hidden from easy view of anyone who might wander past. There was no way he could resist joining in on the sly. He stroked his shaft, letting his gaze roam over her in admiration. Her skin was lighter than his own, yet slightly tanned, the lines from her bikini top clearly marked against her bare flesh. A faint scattering of freckles were there, and he longed to lick his way from one to the next to the next, creating a mosaic of pleasure over her entire body.

Another moan echoed in his ears as she arched hard, nipples pointed skyward. Her pace picked up and he obliged her unspoken direction. Harder, faster. Full measure each time as his fist surrounded his erection with a firm grasp. His gaze remained fixated on her body, on the way her breasts shook as she breathed erratically. The way she tossed her head from side to side, her gasps increasing in volume. As her passion rose, a pulse at the base of his balls began a drumbeat loud enough to deafen him.

"*Ahhh...*"

Her cry pushed him over the edge. Jared cupped his right hand over the head of his cock to stop from spraying all over the barrier between himself and his mysterious angel. Then he stumbled back a quarter pace to lean on the wall and let it hold him vertical, because damn if he remembered how to stand.

"Sweet mercy." The world spun.

They both remained motionless for a full minute. If he'd attempted to move sooner, Jared figured he'd have tripped over his own feet and landed on his ass, cock still hanging from his jeans.

He wiped himself clean and smiled at the woman who'd now slid all the way onto her back, her panting evident from the rocking motions of her torso. She dragged herself upright and blew out a big breath of air.

She pulled on her bra and rearranged the rest of her clothing, turning just enough he had a chance to spot the gorgeous ink on her lower back. Damn, what he wouldn't give to be able to take a closer look. Jared put everything back in place, feeling slightly amused they were so connected—they could have had sex for how well their timing worked out.

But, unfortunately, that wasn't to be. He flipped a salute her direction and slipped out from his hidden alcove. Now he simply had to get going, as much fun as the interlude had been. He strolled down the deck toward the hallway he'd first come out, admiring the mountains on his right, the majestic vista passing rapidly as a strong wind blessed his face.

Jared jerked to a stop and stared in dismay. The mountains *were* moving, more than him glancing past them should make them move. He raced to the railing and clung to it, grip tightening to the point of pain.

There was no gangplank. There was no dock. Nothing but wide-open ocean greeted his frantic search.

While he'd been busy getting off in his little voyeuristic manner, the crew had been busy as well, and the ship had left port.

He was trapped on the cruise ship indefinitely.

3

———

*K*eri made her way down the hallway toward the grand ballroom, lingering sexual frustration hovering like a carrion bird. At some point she would step back over the line between aching need and romping desire, and heaven help anyone caught between her and Mark when she snapped, because it wouldn't be pretty.

But ten days. Surely she could hold off the edge for ten days. She simply had to avoid him completely. Keep away from his addictive scent. If she concentrated hard enough she could do this. Heck, she'd heard of others holding off their mating drive for longer than ten days.

She sighed. The fact that the people in those stories were mainly stronger wolves had probably helped. Yet another reason being in the middle of the pack was a pain in the ass. Not only could more powerful wolves in the hierarchy boss her around, but her own body could as well.

Her wolf shuffled inside, almost...gloating. She slapped the beast down, as far from the surface as she could. Fine. She would do this. Show the lupine hussy the human had hidden depths. Maybe her wrist would get sore from masturbating, but she would not follow through on the mating just because her wolf said so.

Still—what a lousy time to be trapped on the cruise ship.

She wondered what the chances were the gift shop had an array of sex toys to stock up on. But this was a shifter-only cruise. They probably assumed no toys were needed.

Her phone vibrated and she hauled it out, relaxing as she spotted Tessa's name.

"What's shaking, baby?" Keri turned the corner and stood against the wall to allow a group of travelers past her.

"I need help. There's trouble already. I'm so screwed. It's terrible. I want to know if I can quit now and—"

"Tessa. Full stop on the mouth."

"Stopping."

Acting as a troubleshooter was going to require more handholding than she'd imagined. "Are you standing up?"

"No."

"Put the phone down, do ten jumping jacks, then pace while you explain what's wrong." It was the same thing she'd had to deal with back in their college days. Why Tessa thought she had to tie down her cat nature was beyond comprehension.

The scent of food—baked pastries, decadent chocolate and coffee—tugged her by the nose, and Keri slipped into one of the twenty-four-hour restaurants. Shifter-specialty cruising meant there would always be food available to keep up with shifter metabolisms, even more than on board a regular sailing. She eyed the long line of baking offered up like heavenly temptation.

This might be her saving grace while her body waged hormonal war. She would simply stuff herself constantly in an attempt to satisfy one craving with another. Rich, sweet, sticky food. Licking chocolate off her fingers, *mmm*, licking chocolate off Mark. Off the solid muscles of his abdomen before strolling lower and—

Great. So much for food being a distraction. She was horny again.

Her phone crackled and Tessa's much perkier voice rang out. "Back. Thank you for the reminder. Hey, I need you to go escort one of the maintenance men to the Fedoras' suite. They're having issues with a couple little things and want them fixed, but don't want just anyone in there. I assured them we would use the utmost care in their accommodation."

"Hey, no problem. Quick thinking, by the way. You want me to join the guy downstairs or—?"

"Head straight to the suite. Chad is already giving out assignments so by the time you get to their rooms, maintenance should be waiting for you."

"Done and done, and please, can you stay on your feet? You really can do this if you're not trying to pretend to be a desk jockey."

"Deal."

It was too tempting to resist. Keri snagged a chocolate éclair before leaving the restaurant and jogging toward the service elevators. The wait for the ride was better because she had the rich burst of flavour rolling down her throat, creamy and delectable. She stuck the last bit into her mouth just as the doors opened.

A group of staff pushed out as she stepped in. Someone jostled her elbow and she dropped her cell phone. The doors closed to her right as she stooped to pick it up and came eye to eye with a pair of florescent green Crocs. Whitewashed jeans, faded in all the right places, led her gaze upward, the thread-worn patch slightly to the right of his groin showcasing a nice firm package. Hmm, big enough to cause trouble and that was before he got hard.

The trembling in her limbs made it tough to stand. Made it nearly impossible to continue her slow visual scan up past the worker's belt lashed around his hips, to the buttons running up the front of his shirt. One. Two. Three... to where the material gaped open and a plain blue T-shirt showed.

More shaking arrived, as if she were on the verge of a seizure. She knew why—there was no way she couldn't know, not with the aroma in the small quarters making her mouth water and her nipples tighten. The final inches of lifting her gaze were less about confirming she was alone with Mark in the elevator. No, her hesitation was more about giving herself time to resist. To lock her limbs into immobility and refuse the urge to reach out and strip him here and now.

This was the third time they'd met. Surely if they were mates, he'd say something. Do something. Maybe she was wrong? Perhaps she'd hit the wolf equivalent of a hormonal overload and it was all in her head.

All she knew for sure was the ball was in his court. No way would she make the first move, just in case. Because how awkward would that be, to assume someone was your mate and be wrong?

As their eyes met, a nice little daydream flashed through her brain. It started with her punching the emergency stop button, skipped past exactly how they got naked, hesitated and moved in slow motion long enough for her to stab herself on his cock and finished with them both screaming out in orgasm loud enough to scare the dolphins leaping in the waves off the ship's prow.

"Hey." His smile—lethal.

She nodded rapidly, her jaw clenched tight to stop herself from begging for...something. Of course, that meant she didn't actually say anything. Seemed safer. Really. Or she might shout something crude and risqué.

She turned to face the elevator doors, locking her gaze on the thin vertical line between them as if it was the only safe point in the world.

Taking tiny breaths of air through her mouth didn't help—it meant instead of his scent rolling through her brain, his taste mixed with the lingering chocolate on her tongue.

In her peripheral vision his beautiful biceps flexed and her libido fluttered, landing somewhere in her belly and continuing to flap incessantly.

Mark coughed. "I hope you don't think I'm being forward, but there's something we have to do."

He leaned closer and she held her breath.

Ohmygodohmygod.

His body brushed hers briefly as he jabbed one of the elevator buttons. He stepped back and smiled easily. "Works better if you tell it where to go."

The mechanical cage rose slowly. Keri's mouth was full of moisture. She wanted to talk, but was afraid anything she said would be accompanied by a spray of spit. Which would be an oh-so-attractive way to begin, right?

His smile faded slowly as his chin tipped downward. A gentle concern crossed his face with the tiniest bit of a crease between his eyes. It was so adorable she wanted to rub it and make everything better. She swallowed hard, regretting the action immediately as his flavour rushed through her again. Keri closed her eyes and leaned back on the wall. *Don't touch. Don't touch.*

A whisper-soft brush against her cheek made her eyes

fly open. His knuckles finished a slow drag over her skin before he pulled back and showed her dark chocolate on his fingertips.

"You were in a hurry, were you?"

Oh boy. She sucked in her courage and slapped down her wolf. She rammed her hand forward. "Keri Smith."

He hesitated. Was he as reluctant as she was to make personal contact? Yet, why would he be, other than if he was trying to protect her?

Then he lifted his hand and licked the chocolate from his fingers. The warm buzz in her belly slipped a foot lower and attached itself to her clit. She could be wearing a strap-on rabbit-assisted vibrator right now, turned on high, and it wouldn't have as much effect as watching him.

He wiped his hand dry on his shirt and finally wrapped his fingers around hers. "Jar—Mark Weaver. We met in the crew staff room, right?"

"Right."

She stared, mesmerized. With his hair pulled back into a ponytail, his dark, beautiful eyes were center stage. The light creamy brown of his skin turned her thoughts back to chocolate. Bad, evil thoughts she didn't want to have to deal with right now.

But when she retreated from dangerous territory, the only thing that remained was the haunting question of why in the world he hadn't reacted to her? She was one second away from yanking him over and shoving her tongue down his throat.

~

HE WAS TRAPPED. She wasn't letting go. His wolf rubbed beneath his skin so hard Jared thought he might spontaneously shift, and still his intriguing stranger wouldn't release his fingers.

He tugged a little harder. She gasped then jerked herself upright and whipped her amazing green eyes off him. Her hands disappeared behind her like a naughty child caught with her fingers in the cookie jar.

Damn, why'd she have to have a boyfriend? She was adorable, and sexy, and his wolf thought she was fascinating. So much to offer, yet so many barriers between them.

The elevator doors slid open and he gestured her out. She fled—the only word for it. He didn't mind. That meant he got to stare at her ass as she sped down the lush red carpet. Fine. Maybe he couldn't have her, but he could still be nice. Even women with bedmates liked being treated nice, and being a gentleman could be as much fun as having funky monkey sex.

Almost.

Kinda.

Not really, but oh well.

She stopped before oversized double doors, and he decided it was time to turn on the charm. The "just friends even though you deserve more" charm that left women feeling like a million bucks.

"So, one of the fancy suites. Nice. Bet it's got more room than my two-by-four space."

Keri knocked before answering. "Probably more room than yours, mine and twenty staff quarters shoved together."

She talked to the floor. He examined the area by her feet. Nothing there.

Okay...

There was no response to her second knock either, so she pulled a pass card from her pocket and let them in.

Jared glanced around in appreciation. Not only luxurious, the place was bright with sunlight. "Sweet. I love the windows. Hate the tiny things downstairs. I'd rather rig a hammock on the deck and sleep under the stairs than stay trapped in that lower berth."

Keri nodded. "I hear you. My room is better than yours, but nothing like this."

He waited. When he'd checked in as required at eleven, Chad had informed him he was on the maintenance crew, then grudgingly found a work belt for him when he admitted to having "forgotten" his at home. Putting Chad's sigh of disgust aside, since it had been deserved this time, the job placement came as a huge relief. He had to continue with the charade until he found a way off the ship, but if it had turned out his pack mate had been hired to cook, or worse, entertain? Jared would have been shit-outta-luck.

Fixing squeaky doors he could do.

But Keri wasn't telling him what specifically needed to be done. She was alternating between staring at the floor and sneaking glances at him.

His wolf rumbled again as he caught a peek into her big wide eyes. *Yes, damn beast, I get the message. You like her. Down, boy.* He and his wolf struggled for dominance in a way he'd never experienced before. Then the wild part inside him retreated—almost pouting—into the corner.

Being a wolf had never been so weird.

Time to get this show on the road. Or ocean, or whatever. Jared rubbed his hands together. "What's first on the agenda?"

Keri jerked to attention. "Oh, right. Taps in the master bathroom sink are dripping."

"Master bathroom? Man, now I'm really jealous."

The suite went on and on, glistening gold and shining

silver contrasting with the lavish textiles. Keri pressed open a door and stood aside. Jared forced himself to the far side of the doorway to avoid rubbing their bodies together, even though he really, *really* would have liked to do some rubbing.

The taps were an easy fix, although her watching his every move made it a little more nerve-racking.

"You trying to learn a new trade?" He glanced up from his wrench. Her cheeks were flushed red, and she seemed to have the hardest time looking away from him.

"What?" She shook herself and blinked hard.

Erratic breathing, little gasps escaping her lips. She'd wrapped her arms around her waist, her breasts framed by her arms. Her fingers rubbed her skin above her beltline, fidgeting. Even if he hadn't seen her orgasm only a little while ago, he still would have recognized the signs.

She was turned on.

Sweet mercy. He had to get this back to safe territory. "I said I wondered if you were studying to learn a new trade, you know, with how closely you're taking notes."

She stuttered then backed away from the door. "I'm sorry, that was rude. No, well, I do have to keep an eye on you. Not that I don't trust you, but the suite belongs to the Fedoras, and so they're a little fussy about who gets to come in, and that kind of thing."

Jared whistled to cover his shock. *Oh hello, bad news.* "Fedoras? As in the British royal werewolf Fedoras?"

"Right. They're traveling with a couple bodyguards, but otherwise it's all rather low-key. They seem very nice."

Sure. Nice for anyone who wasn't trying to avoid meeting up with people like them.

This entire cruise-entrapment thing got better and better by the minute. *Not.*

"That's...cool. So, we'll be seeing them on the ship? I mean, the normal people will see them, not us slaves hiding in the background."

She laughed, an honest, real laugh, and some of the tension in the air disappeared. "We're not going to chain you to the wall in your room when you're not on duty. The Arctic Wolf Cruise Lines is pretty good about allowing crew time to enjoy the view as well. We're all shifters, we understand the need to have some fun."

"Thank you for that." He tested the taps, turning them off and on a few times as he pretended to ensure the drip was gone. Actually, it took a lot of strength to not blurt out he'd be okay with chains in his room if she were the one putting them on him.

Concentrate. Job. Then dire necessities like buying some clothes to get him through this farce. Only now he'd have to avoid meeting any of the passengers while shopping just in case. What a mess.

He picked up his tools and pivoted, stopping in confusion when he discovered Keri was staring again, her face twisted into a frightened expression. She seemed so uncomfortable around him.

A horrible, terrible thought struck. "Keri? Your boyfriend, Chad?"

"My boyfriend?" She blinked. "Um, yeah, Chad. What about him?"

Jared moved slowly. He'd seen someone act this way before, kind of like a terrified rabbit. He took her hand in his and curled his fingers around her cold digits. "He's not the jealous type, is he? I mean, you're not going to be in trouble because you're here alone with me? Because you..."

She looked ready to fall over. "I, what?"

What did he say? Offer her safe keeping? Suggest she

consider her options? *You don't have to be with him, I'll take care of you* flashed into his brain, and he snapped his mouth shut before the words could escape.

She was a grown wolf, with a mind of her own, but there were times even a wolf could get into a situation they didn't know how to get out of. "Just wanted you to remember you don't have to be with anyone who doesn't treat you right. If you're having any issues, you can always go to the closest Alpha. Back in Haines, my Alpha Keil is—"

"No, no wait, you don't understand." Her instant denial made another thread of suspicion flare. She pulled herself back to calm in an incredibly quick amount of time. "That's very sweet of you, but no. I'm not in any trouble. And Chad isn't giving me any grief, really. I mean." She wrinkled her nose. "Nothing I can't handle."

Jared nodded slowly. "Okay."

Keri stepped back and smiled brightly. "Well, next fix? The closet door. This way."

Her forced perky tone grated on his nerves. Whatever else was going on, that deception alone was a clear sign she wasn't telling him the whole truth.

Still, not much he could do at this moment. He stepped quickly after her into the bedroom. Her sudden stop came far sooner than he expected, and he slammed directly into her backside.

She fell forward, and Jared tried to save them both. He snagged his fingers on her belt and together they teetered off-balance for a split second. It was no use, gravity won. They twisted and landed with a soft grunt on the bed. Keri was trapped under him, and he felt every inch of her smooth muscles, her ass soft under his groin. He rolled off her as if she were on fire.

Damn it. Last thing she needed if she had a jerk for a

boyfriend was to have a strange wolf's scent all over her.

He rolled too far and bumped into the headboard. The intricate built-in bookcase rocked forward, and jewelry and books fell on top of him.

"Shit. I'm sorry."

She scrambled over and levered the unit back to vertical before helping pick items off him. "My fault. I didn't...I wasn't thinking."

"Here. Let me help."

He moved to replace the books, but she shook her head. "Not going to work. Just leave it in a pile and I'll explain what happened."

Was she going to be in trouble because of him? "I'll explain. It was my fault. Don't let them fire you over this, okay?"

She sat on the edge of the bed and smiled weakly. "You don't have to worry about me being fired. But if you could fix the door, please? I should get going on a few other things."

Jared headed to the closet sheepishly. Some help he was. Making more work for her, on top of the issues she had to deal with. He adjusted the door while watching her out of the corner of his eye as she tidied the best she could. Her entire demeanor screamed something was wrong. The way she kept stealing glances at him—he vowed then and there he was going to look out for her. Not only because his wolf demanded it, but because he kind of liked her. She had spunk.

And if there was anything fishy going on with Chad...

Jared might not be the strongest wolf around, but he wasn't willing to let anyone suffer. Especially not someone he was interested in. Far more interested in than seemed logical.

4

———

essa dragged her around the running track for another loop and Keri groaned. "Aren't we done yet?"

"Someone smart told me to let the cat nature out. Trust me, I need this. You're gonna need this."

Three days. Three long, lonely, tormented days. Keri had managed to avoid any further direct contact with *him*, even attempting to stop thinking of him. The gift shop had no toys, but happily the tiny bathroom in her cabin had a removable showerhead that was saving her from developing carpel tunnel. The mating urge had settled to a constant throb, as if her entire body were one giant mosquito bite, rubbed with poison ivy then sprinkled with itching powder.

It was actually far more bearable than she'd expected.

Of course, her concentration levels had dropped. She'd managed to avoid giving any too-weird advice, mainly because Tessa had totally picked up the ball and was rocking the job hard. She hadn't had a single panic attack in the past twenty-four hours, luckily for Keri.

Troubleshooting right now would require more mental power than she could muster.

The surface under their feet passed smoothly, the soles of their runners smacking the track with a steady *slap, slap, slap*. The even rhythm calmed her and slowly the edge of sexual urgency dulled enough she could take a full breath.

All around them were signs this wasn't your typical Alaskan cruise. A giant grizzly lumbered past on all fours, two cougars sprinted on the far side of the track, their tawny fur a blur of motion. A loud scream of satisfaction rose as one crossed the imaginary finish line a body length ahead of the other.

Keri wanted to smile and soak it all in, to enjoy the sheer joy of being a shifter. If she wasn't so damn horny, life would be wonderful.

Finally Tessa led them to the stretching mats. Outside the long row of floor-to-ceiling windows, the ocean waves broke against the shore of the small islands the ship passed. The sky was grey today, the horizon and the water's surface blending in the distance to give the illusion of an endless waterway rising heavenward.

Keri sank to the floor and groaned as her tight muscles protested being flexed. "Right now I hate you, but thanks for hauling my ass out. I needed that."

Beside her, Tessa cranked out sit-ups, one after another, her voice barely changing as she spoke. "You might need something more than a workout in a minute. This is completely hush-hush, but there's been trouble."

"Something wrong?" Couldn't be too bad, since Tessa wasn't spazzing like a cat tossed in a swimming pool.

"We have a thief on the ship."

"Really?" Keri turned to face her friend full-on. "You've had reports of missing stuff?"

Tessa nodded. "The first couple were mentioned as 'we're not sure if we've misplaced it, can we look in the lost and found?' But there are too many now for it to be a coincidence."

Oh, this was bad. "Big stuff, small stuff?"

"Easy-to-grab things of value. Watches and jewelry left on counters."

Keri stared in surprise at her friend. "Why didn't you tell me sooner?"

Tessa snapped to a sitting position and grinned sheepishly. "You mean why didn't I freak out on you sooner?"

Kinda. "Aren't you worried?"

A long sigh escaped Tessa. "I'm past worried. Now I'm mad. But I didn't tell you because the advice you gave me at the start of the trip was right. I knew what to do. I handled it —I calmed people down and checked the usual systems. But it's gotten to the point we need to find out what is going on or there will be trouble. I don't want this cruise to be remembered as the one with the petty thief."

Keri agreed. "Well, good for you for starting strong, and I'll do what I can. You have any suspicions?"

A small shrug. "Chad thought the only similarity between—"

"Chad?" Another person she'd been totally avoiding, because trying to explain his touch was now enough to trigger a gag reflex? Tough, not without spilling the beans on her mate being on board. Yet the man was relentless— she hadn't had to duck into any closets to avoid him, but it had been close. "You've talked to Chad about this?"

"He's the one who reported the first items to me. The head of the housekeeping department has been all over him with news. Often enough that he felt the need to bend his hoity-toity attitude and report to me." Tessa rested a hand on Keri's shoulder. "I wasn't keeping secrets from you, and certainly not keeping them to share with Chad."

A rush of heat raced over Keri's face. This was awkward. "Not as if you have to report to me or anything. And you and him have lots in common, after all. Family friend forever, etc., etc."

"Please. Think about it. Me and Chad? Gack. He's like the most doggy wolf I've ever met."

"Hey, some girls have a thing for their older brother's best friend." Tessa screwed up her face into the most hideous grimace, and Keri laughed. "Okay, yes, I know you've said before he's not your type."

"Totally. Besides, I thought you and he were making googly eyes at each other. Did you find someone else who's keeping you busy in your cabin for hours on end?"

Keri didn't think her time away had been for long enough to be noticed. Good thing her excessive water usage couldn't be traced. "No, no one. But tell me more about this crow in our midst. What was Chad's observation?"

Tessa stepped close to the window and peered out. "He wonders if someone in maintenance might be involved."

Keri's stomach fell, bounced off the floor and rebounded into her throat. "Maintenance?" she squeaked.

"So far most reports have occurred sometime after one of the crew went to do a job. And Keri?" Tessa wrinkled her nose as she turned, shoulders resting against the glass. "The Fedoras asked if you happened to spot a brooch when you were in their suite the other day. They put back the things that fell when the bookcase shifted position, but Mrs. Fedora only noticed today she can't find her diamond-and-ruby brooch."

Panic rushed through Keri like a shot of neat tequila,

numbing even as it loosened her tongue. "I didn't take anything."

Tessa frowned. "Of course you didn't. But we need to figure this out. I don't want to have to call in the police at any of our ports of call. There's the shifter-only issue, plus the cruise line doesn't need any negative publicity."

Keri backpedaled fast. "Definitely not. No worries. I mean, yes, worries, but we can deal with this. I mean, I'll try. I mean..."

Babbling. Not good.

Her friend raised one brow high, suspicion all over her face. "What aren't you telling me?"

"Me? Nothing. Everything is fine. Thanks for the run and, gee, look at the time." Keri snapped her wrist up in front of her face.

She wasn't wearing a watch.

Tessa snorted. "If I didn't know better, I'd think you had a hot date or something. You sure are acting weird."

If she was going to get out of this without the legendary cat curiosity pulling everything out one secret at a time, Keri needed her best academy performance, and now.

"Sorry. It's nothing..." Time for a new tactic. Redirection. "...but can I say how impressed I am? It's as if you're a different cat than the one who nearly shook me apart that first day. I'm proud of you for not panicking."

"Thanks, but I'm not sure if it's because I've become resigned to the trip being a disaster and I'm simply 'whatever', or if I've reached a magical point of nirvana and just trust it will work out."

Keri pointed out the window at the crowds playing and relaxing on the deck below them. There were couples reclined on deck chairs, sipping drinks. People lawn bowling. A group of wolves in furry form batted a ball around while a half-dozen big cats lay draped over railings and in specialized hammocks, their enormous paws twitching as they slept.

"That doesn't look like a disaster to me. Looks like a lot of people having fun, thrilled to be here. We'll deal with the thefts, I promise."

Tessa lifted her hand, knuckles outward. "You're the bestest."

Keri returned their usual salute, making a huge effort to appear perky and positive. "Let me know what else you hear, okay? I'm going to grab a shower. See you at supper?"

"Save you a seat."

They left the track area in opposite directions, Tessa toward her office, Keri supposedly toward her room. But the instant she rounded the corner out of her friend's sight, she turned. Raced down a side stairwell that led to the lowest levels of the ship and the crew quarters.

What the heck was her mate up to? Was he really a thief?

She stared at his cabin door for a full minute debating what she was about to do. It wasn't breaking and entering—she had full permission to access the staff quarters on the ship. But the fact she was going in because she suspected he'd...

No. She wasn't even going to think it. She wasn't. It was bad enough to wonder how they would manage everything else, like where to live and meeting each other's families, and which pack to join and what all, without also speculating if her mate was used to spending time behind bars.

Keri screwed up her courage and knocked loudly.

When there was no answer, she glanced both directions

down the hallway then used her pass card and slipped into his room.

First impression—her knees nearly gave way as his scent hit her fully for the first time in days. The lingering aroma made her mouth water, and all her beaten-down lusts sprang up with an energizer-bunny enthusiasm.

She clung to the wall and closed her eyes as she brought her body back under control. This exploration of his room was for not only their sakes as future partners, but Tessa's as well. If Mark was stealing, she could replace the items as soon as possible, and they could move on from here. She'd tie his ass to the bed for the duration of the trip if she had to —and didn't that lovely mental image bring on more hot flashes—but she'd keep him out of jail and allow the cruise to finish up positively.

It took a moment, but Keri pulled it together. Surprisingly, it was her wolf who provided the strength she needed. The beast was chomping at the bit to get out, but instead of frustration the strongest sensation was approval. A sense of peace poured from the beast at being enveloped with her mate's scent. Keri breathed out slowly, and her wolf rumbled in satisfaction, content for the first time in days.

Like she was waiting.

Keri shook her head. Being a shifter was cool, but confusing. The wolf was her, and she was the wolf, but there were times the lupine side made no sense to the human brain.

A quick peek around the room showed nothing unusual, so Keri moved to explore more thoroughly. She opened the closet, surprised to find how little clothing hung there. The green Crocs she'd seen him wear were on the floor next to a brand-new gym bag. The threadbare jeans he'd looked so yummy in that first day hung next to a shirt. A price tag from the ship's shop dangled from the sleeve.

There was nothing else. No coat, no extra clothing. Keri opened dresser drawers and found a couple packages of underwear, a package of socks and a T-shirt, also tagged from the onboard store. The receipt lay next to them, and she looked closer at the sale items listed.

One pair of pants, the shirt, a pair of runners. Toothpaste and toothbrush. Package of razors. Shampoo and soap. A gym bag.

Had he not brought a single thing onto the ship with him?

She remembered the running man back on the dockside, and once again considered if Mark could have been him. But why had he stayed on the ship?

The lack of clothing was suspicious, but as she searched further, there were no signs of any jewelry. Nothing hidden anywhere—with so little in the room that detail was simple enough to ascertain.

He wasn't the thief, or he'd hidden the items elsewhere. Regardless, there was something fishy going on.

Keri looked longingly at the bed. The sheets were rumpled, his half-assed attempt at straightening the covers leaving it borderline messy. She gave into her longings and ditched her shoes. Her own scent was everywhere so he would already know she'd been in his quarters. Maybe a clear message would be enough to make him smarten up if he was involved in something illegal. A "don't look now, but I'm watching you" message.

Oh, bullshit. She wasn't trying to pass on any warning, she just wanted to root around in his bed for a minute to drive herself crazy. She crawled under the top sheet and pulled it over her head, surrounding herself in his scent like a kid diving into a swimming pool. The itching, aching, pulsing need of her wolf soothed and heated at the same time. She needed to have him come and strip her down. To bury his face between her legs and lick her until she screamed. Needed to feel him mount over her and take her, to feel his teeth sink into her flesh as he claimed her.

Keri let the sensation overwhelm her as she lay panting with desire. Only one minute more, then she'd pull herself away and get on with her search for the thief.

JARED CURSED as he attempted to wiggle farther under the sink. Stupid cruise ships with their teeny tiny bathrooms. Stupid fucking cruise ships with their never-ending list of maintenance jobs, of which he seemed to get all the shitty ones—and he knew exactly who to thank for that.

Three days. He'd been stuck on this ship for three bloody days, and so far there hadn't been any decent chance for him to escape.

The first time they'd made port he'd been tangled up with another couple of the crew repairing the pumps on the swimming pool, which luckily he knew how to fix. Unluckily, he was the only one who did, so it wasn't as if he could abandon the other guys and flee to shore. Even though it was tempting to escape and book a ride back to Haines on a speedboat—heck, he'd buy himself a boat to get home if he had to—the others in maintenance were on the ship for a real job. They needed the money, and he wasn't going to make them lose needed wages.

His damn martyr complex had turned this accidental excursion into a hell of a lot more work than he'd done for years. Coupled with the fact he'd rubbed Chad's ass the wrong way that first day…

Yeah, the ability to make friends and influence people, he had it. His parents always warned him that his quirky sense of humour was going to get him in trouble someday, and it seemed *someday* had arrived. Chad personally escorted him to the dirtiest jobs and subtly gloated how if *Mark* was fortunate and worked hard, maybe someday he too could be one of the upper class and not the slave labour.

Jared wanted to buy the bloody cruise ship and shove it up Chad's upper-class ass.

So now they were on day four, nearly halfway through the cruise, and he wondered if it was even worth trying to ditch the ship. The work sucked, he missed his coffee maker, but if he left, there was another concern to think about, also involving Chad.

Keri.

He'd watched her from a distance when he could. Which was creepy as all get out in a way, and not totally his idea. He was uneasy about Keri, and making sure there was nothing bad going on with Chad was important. But more than that, stalking her in his few spare moments was the only way he could make his wolf happy enough to get any rest at all. The creature was insistent they go drop in on the woman. Maybe shred a few layers of clothing off her body. Put a real smile on her face—and his wolf had resorted to making the images popping to mind as specific as possible, which was totally dirty pool on the beast's part.

His wolf wanted the woman, or more correctly the woman's wolf, with something close to obsession.

Keri wasn't happy. When she smiled, it never reached her eyes. And while he hadn't been around all the time, he'd seen enough to notice that the few times he'd had her under observation, she'd ducked away from Chad like he was bad business.

Had they had a lovers' spat?

Jared didn't trust the guy. Seemed the type to take things out on a girl to get what he wanted.

There was nothing to be done about it now but wait out the rest of the voyage. At least he was due some time off—the schedule clearly put him free for the rest of the day after he finished this job. Even slave master Chad couldn't change the master calendar without approval and paying overtime. Which the asshole wouldn't do because Jared suspected the extra cash would be considered a wonderful thing.

Jared cranked the wrench a little harder. Yup. This afternoon he was going to go find a quiet place on deck and suntan. Sleep. Maybe buy a beer and chill…

Ah, who was he kidding? He was going to have a shower, jerk off—*again*, then find Keri and try to silently follow her. Again.

Obsessed. It wasn't just the beast who had it bad.

He tightened the bolt one more time, and the upper arm of the pipes broke apart, cold water spraying everywhere. A shot struck him directly in the eyes, and he grasped blindly for the water shut-off.

By the time he'd managed to stop the spray, he was soaked, and his only moderately dry item, his work pants, he used on the puddle at his feet. Jared sat forlornly on the floor, wishing he was five and could enjoy a good pout. Damn cruise ship. Damn water taps.

He chuckled. *Poor baby Jared.* He snapped himself out of his funk, sopped up the floor and put things into place the best he could before using his walkie-talkie.

"Sorry, guys, the master line snapped. Someone needs to bring extra parts to replace it."

One of the team he'd worked with earlier responded quickly. "I can finish it up for you. It's your afternoon off. Which room you in?"

Jared told him then looked down at himself. "If I leave my wet stuff here, can you take it for me?"

His co-worker laughed. "You did that good a job, did you? No worries. I'll bring a cart with me to clean up. I'll hang your things in the staff-room bath."

"Awesome. I'm heading back to my quarters for dry gear. I don't think the passengers would appreciate seeing me streaking with a pile of dripping clothing soaking the carpets in my wake."

"Yeah, the carpets would be tough to explain to management."

Jared tucked his wet things into the tub before shifting to wolf. He could probably have walked the halls naked—most shifters were pretty cool about stuff like that—but he wasn't sure of the exact rules regarding crew and passengers, and at this point, it wasn't as if he wanted any extra attention his direction. Walking in his wolf form? No one would take a second glance.

He grabbed his work belt in his mouth. That was the one item he couldn't afford to leave behind. Chad would probably charge him triple to replace it if anything went missing. It wasn't the money; it was the gloating Jared couldn't stand to anticipate.

He got himself out of the room and trotted downward, taking the stairs, slipping past the restaurants and games rooms. Something wonderful was being cooked for lunch, and he paused to enjoy the rich aroma on the air.

Hmmm. Dry clothes, lunch, *then* stalking.

With his entire afternoon schedule planned, he resumed the trip into the depths of the ship and his cabin. The wonderful smell of lunch faded, only to be replaced by something else even more mouthwatering. Jared sped up, the tools in his belt jingling as he trotted forward, following the most incredible scent he'd ever experienced. It made his fur stand on end and all kinds of happy little pheromones leap to life.

Every step increased his need. His eagerness to discover what exactly was before him drove him to a near run. He only slowed enough to stop the tools from shaking free from the tool belt and smacking him in the face.

Incredibly, the trail of scent led directly to his cabin door. He lowered himself to the floor and sniffed cautiously. A cloud of the most potent aphrodisiac surrounded him, and he barely contained his howl of delight.

His mate?

Was that scent tantalizing him really his mate?

His wolf side roared to life and urged him to get his ass in gear. He shifted back to human, and his ability to smell cut off abruptly, as usual. The lack of olfactory input in this form allowed him to control his hands enough to sneak his room card from his tool belt and undo the lock.

Jared pushed the heavy door open and stared into Keri's wide eyes as she sat in the middle of his bed, tangled in the sheets.

5

Her tongue wasn't where it was supposed to be.

In the five seconds since the door had begun to open—heart-attack type symptoms electrifying her body as she sprang up to face whoever was about to discover her doing unexplainable things to a crew member's bed—she had opened her mouth to scream then stopped when her mate's now-familiar face came into view.

Something still felt odd. Her brain seemed to bubble and froth until comprehension finally sank in. Her tongue? She must have swallowed it. There certainly was something stuck in her throat as he stood with one arm holding the door open, his naked body framed in the opening like an erotic work of art.

Naked. *Oh my.*

She started at his toes and worked her way up. While he'd been impressive in his jeans, he did naked even better. There was an incredible look to a naked wolf—the cut of their muscles slightly sharper than cat or bear shifters. And *my, oh my,* she was appreciative of all his muscles. Fixated on them, in fact. Engrossed in the way his thigh muscles flexed as he stepped into the room. Her gaze trickled upward, and that damn tongue stuck in her throat got in the way again as she attempted to swallow. He was...more than sufficient above the thighs as well.

A sharp cough sounded at the same moment the door clicked shut.

She was mesmerized, staring at his groin.

Oh my, oh my, oh my.

Muscles flexed again as he knelt, his head replacing the level her eyes were stuck at. When his smile flashed into view, the constriction around her throat eased slightly.

"Hi." The word squeaked out. One word seemed to be her maximum output right now.

His grin widened. "This is the kind of room service I've been longing for. But if you don't mind...I have one thing I need to double-check."

She watched in confusion as he placed a tool belt—*why is he naked, but carrying a tool belt?*—on the side table beside the bed. Then he shifted into his wolf and leapt up next to her.

He was dark grey, lean in his body with beautiful markings on his chest. He brushed his soft fur against her arm, and she moved to give him more room. When he stuck his muzzle next to her ear and took a deep breath, her own wolf shivered mightily.

At this point she didn't care what he was double-checking as long as it involved him shifting back soon and doing her hard and fast. All thoughts of holding out any longer were tossed out the small porthole window. He was her mate, she was in his bed, and damn the consequences. Thievery, cruises, best friends. All the details of her human concerns evaporated, replaced with a hunger that was mostly animalistic.

She grabbed the bottom of her T-shirt and stripped it off. By the time she'd wiggled out of her jeans, he'd shifted back, his sexy grin settling into something between astonishment and violent hunger.

"You're my mate." The wonder in his voice made her smile.

"Yes."

"Why didn't you tell me?" He cupped her face, his thumb stroking her cheek.

Keri paused. "You didn't know?"

His gaze dropped to her mouth. "I know now."

He leaned closer, just a tiny bit, and Keri's heart flipped. The brush of air from his lips caressed past like a butterfly wing a split second before they made contact.

Sticking a finger into an electric socket would be boring from now on. Not that she often played with electricity, but those old cartoons flashing every bone highlighted when... She lost her train of thought as his tongue slicked over her bottom lip.

She melted into a happy puddle of puddleness, catching hold of his shoulders and pulling him over her, mouths staying in contact. She shook with need, but he pinned her with his weight and held her in place, one hand still cupping her face and restraining her as he kissed her senseless.

Tongue. Teeth. Lips. Air. It was all a tangle of sensation and yearning, and there was nothing she wanted more at this moment than to kiss him forever. Between her legs a heavy ache pulsed, but even that could be ignored for a minute because kissing her mate was unlike anything she'd ever experienced before.

Climaxes? Wild sexual romps? She was a wolf and had had her fair share over the years, but those experiences blurred into some half-forgotten story—like the assigned reading she had of *Moby Dick* during school. It was about someone chasing something and there was a harpoon involved, but the rest of the details were fuzzy.

He rolled onto his back and dragged her over him. Suddenly she was reading the freaking Coles Notes and it all made sense, especially the harpoon bit. Another slide of his tongue followed. His fingers braided through her hair as he tugged and arranged her to his liking.

Her thighs straddled his waist, his erection solid against her belly, and the tingles shot harder. Keri planted one hand on either side of his head and forced her lips away from his. The light in his eyes was to die for.

"Hi." His gaze dropped to her lips and he outlined them again. "You taste good."

A growl broke loose unintentionally and his grin widened.

Yeah, the slow was nice, but she wanted more than nice. She wanted some screaming and stomping and…

She leaned down and kissed his neck, and this time he was the one who rumbled. She nipped lightly, and he snapped upright a foot, strong abdominal muscles under her shooting them both vertical. "Oh God, woman. You ready for this?"

"For my mate?" Keri's brain wasn't attached to anything but the sensual points of her body. "Is anyone? You worried?"

"No. I'm yours, you're mine. I'm free and clear, and well over twenty-one, and if I'm not inside you in about thirty seconds I'm going to die." He followed up by digging his teeth into her neck and pinning her in place while he stripped off her bra.

Thirty seconds were going to be far too long,

"I'm yours. I know you thought—" Oh hell, he ripped her panties apart at the hip, and suddenly explaining that Chad wasn't really a boyfriend slipped off the agenda and flashed to ashes faster than taking a blow torch to a scrap of floss.

Keri lifted her hips, and her mate brushed his fingers along her sex and dipped in. When he circled her clit, as if he was going to get her off first, she took matters into her own hands, grasped his erect cock and pressed the wide head between her folds.

"Argggh" or something close to it escaped his lips.

Keri planted her hands on his shoulders and stared into his eyes as she sank and joined them together.

Full, stretched, expanding to fill not only her body but to wrap around her soul and fill her there as well. It was a rush and a thrill and just the way it could be with wolves, and heck if she was going to complain things were happening too fast. She lifted and lowered once before he wrapped his arms around her and kissed her madly again.

If he didn't slow them down he was going to spill right then and there. It was bad enough she'd hogtied him, and they were already having sex. He'd never taken a woman without making sure she'd experienced pleasure, and this was his mate.

Mate, oh freaky day, he was having sex with his *mate*.

Going slow—nice idea, but the reality of their wolves and the lingering scent of her in his brain crumpled that note and tossed it to the side. Slow would happen later. Maybe tomorrow. Or next week. Next week might be possible.

Still, he had to deal with the building pressure because flipping her over and pounding her through the mattress wouldn't be the romantic first time he figured most women wanted. He twisted them until his feet hit the floor, kissing her cheek, licking her neck before taking possession of her mouth and soaking in her taste the best he could.

His lack of smell had always been a pain, but this? Better than he'd expected. She snuck into his system as he kissed her. Slow, but insistent—overwhelming his physical lack with sheer potency.

He slipped his hands between their bodies to cup her breasts, thumbs taking her nipples captive. Commanding them to attention before he pushed her back. Keri arched, and he covered one firm peak with his mouth, then the other. Sucking hard, licking lightly. She wiggled and ground over his cock, her sex coating him with heat and moisture.

Maybe the whole *do it now* thing was going to be okay.

Then she caught his ear in her teeth and bit, and his mind fled.

He rose to his feet, her ass cradled in his hands. She instinctively wrapped her legs around him, but it only took two steps for him to find the door and press her against it. She clung to his shoulders as he lifted her then plunged in deep.

The door creaked and groaned nearly as loud as they did.

"Oh, Mark, that feels *good*." Keri caught the back of his neck and yanked his mouth back to hers, and he forgot everything except fucking them both into oblivion. One thrust after another followed, their teeth knocking, noses bumping. A mad dash of sex and loud noises and all he could feel was her around him. Capturing and claiming him. He adjusted his angle slightly and she squeaked as he hit her clit, and he smiled.

And did it again.

Three more thrusts and she sang out in delight before planting her teeth against his shoulder and biting down.

"Keri...oh, hell yeah." Jared shook off the weakness that threatened to buckle his knees and fought for one last plunge before he gave in to his climax and emptied.

In his mind, words sounded. A feminine tone. A very satisfied feminine tone. *"Oh my goodness."*

Jared leaned heavily against her and smiled. Incredible. *"Keri?"*

She tightened under him, pinned to the wall like a butterfly. *"Is...is that you?"*

The mate connection swirled around them. Something more than physical, something beyond his wildest dreams. Jared focused as hard as possible but there were too many things happening at once to do anything but struggle to remain vertical. *"It's me. Give me a minute."*

Keri's face was buried against his neck, their hearts still pounding. She hadn't loosened the death grip of her legs, thank goodness, or he might have dropped her.

One more minute brought him to the point he could move. He stood, his cock slipping from her body. He carried her carefully back to the bed and lowered her to the messy sheets. Crawled beside her, staring into her eyes, seeing the flush on her cheeks—he focused on her lips, and she moistened them and gazed back with a happy expression.

He tried it again, the speaking-into-her-mind thing that only mates could do. *"Hi, love."*

Her face lit up like a moonrise over the mountain. *"Hi. Are you...happy?"*

Jared laughed. "I'm ecstatic. I'm sorry I didn't know sooner. You must have thought I was being an ass."

Her fingers tangled in his hair. She shook her head. "I didn't understand why you weren't following me around. I figured maybe it had something to do with Chad."

Ick. "You're not...you weren't..."

Her answer rushed out. "No. He's just a friend of the family. I'm yours."

Damn right. "And I'm yours."

Keri lowered her lashes for a moment. "Typical wolf situation though—we have tons of stuff to share, like family backgrounds and everything. Not that I'm worried, because, I mean, we are wolves. I assume we can make things work since that side seems pretty pleased right now."

"More than pleased." Jared lay beside her, his body touching hers at as many points as possible. His wolf was gloating, bloody beast, but he couldn't muster the energy to be offended. "And we'll have a nice long talk. About everything."

Including the bits about him not being Mark but someone else. Only he didn't think, mates or not, that conversation should happen when he was naked.

Female wolves had too good a sense of justice, and he kinda liked the idea of getting to use his balls for a bit longer, now that he'd found her and all.

"How about after a shower? Then I'll buy you lunch and we can talk about anything you like." Jared traced a finger down her body. He adjusted position and bumped the side table hard enough his tool belt fell to the floor. He cursed and went to roll over, but she beat him to it, crawling over top of him and reaching toward the floor. Hmm, nice. Maybe they shouldn't leave quite yet...

"Sounds marvelous. We can go to the—oh, hell." Keri jerked to a stop in mid-sentence.

He curled up beside her to see what was wrong. "What's the matter?"

She had his tool belt in one hand, suspended just off the floor, her eyes wide in near panic.

"You okay? What happened?" He pulled the belt from her fingers and dropped it to the side, up against the mattress. He quickly turned her hands over. "Did you cut yourself?"

She swallowed hard before a smile spread over her face. A sickly smile, forced and unnatural. "I'm fine. Just fine. Everything is fine."

"Keri?" In the last thirty seconds, something had gone terribly wrong.

"Shower. Shower is fine." She scrambled off the bed and toward the teeny enclosure.

The disappointment he felt as she walked away didn't stop him from noticing the incredible tattoo on her lower back. He'd love to check it out more thoroughly—heck, he'd planned on doing a little more playing before actually taking her to the shower, but with her sudden change of mood, he wasn't sure what to do.

He followed her to the doorway of the tiny room. She'd turned on the water and already stood under the spray. There was barely space in the doorless enclosure for her, let alone him beside her, so he leaned on the doorframe and stared to his heart's content, even as he puzzled over her rapid mood change.

She turned her face fully under the water, and he watched the rivulets stream over her skin, down the curve of her neck and over the spot where he'd bit her. He couldn't resist touching the place, his fingers lightly tracing the mark. Keri turned to him and his heart swelled with…love?

This mate thing was a built-in part of them as shifters. She was a piece of him now, and having her tense and upset over some unvoiced matter hurt. He wanted, no, needed to have her happy.

And while this probably wasn't the best time to share that his presence on the ship was unauthorized—there was another issue he could clear up rather quickly. "Keri? I'm glad I found you. And I'm sorry about not knowing. I have a bit of a secret you need to hear—"

Her eyes widened, shining with hope and a bit of sadness.

Sadness?

"You can tell me anything, Mark. I'm your mate, and I promise to support you through anything."

The sheer determination in her voice was curious, but he was distracted by the Mark/Jared thing. "You can't tell anyone, please?"

She squared her shoulders. "I will do what is best for us, for you, even if it's difficult."

"It's not really my fault, you see." Jared dragged a hand through his hair and wanted to slap himself for starting this now. He was still naked and she was right freaking there and naked, and he was rambling about what wasn't the most important issue they had? "Never mind."

Keri caught his hands in hers. She stared him directly in the eye and squeezed his fingers, water rebounding off her shoulders and covering his with a fine mist. "I am your mate. And whatever it is that troubles you, I'm there to help you get out of it. No matter what the reason, I won't abandon you."

Okaaaay…

After her little support-you-through-anything spiel, he was a trifle discombobulated. What did she think he was going to share? That he liked to bathe in moose blood under a full moon?

"I can't smell." The words shot out.

Her jaw dropped.

He hurried on. "In my human form. I smell fine in my wolf, which is why I finally figured out that we were mates. But all those times earlier? I wasn't ignoring you on purpose." He thought back through all their encounters and felt like kicking his own ass. "Man, you must have thought I was a total jerk. I'm so sorry."

Her changing expressions were nearly comical. Shock, bewilderment, a glimmer of understanding and then a smile, although one that barely reached her eyes. "That makes a lot more sense now. I didn't think you were a jerk, although I was confused." She glanced at the walls nearly bumping her on either side. "You know what? Let's go to my suite. The shower is bigger and we can talk for as long as we need."

Jared grabbed his towel and held it up as she stepped out, all wet and slick, and holy moly he wanted to jump her again this second. He wrapped the fabric around her, his knuckles skimming the tops of her breasts as he tucked the ends of the towel in.

She laughed. "What was that sigh for?"

"Did I sigh? God, woman, what you're doing to me."

Keri stepped back and pointed. "You rinse off then come find me. I need to make a few arrangements so we can spend the rest of the day together."

The involuntary drop of her gaze over his body didn't do anything to slow the blood flow to his cock. He caught her fingers in his hand and kissed her knuckles briefly, somehow managing to not drag her back into his arms. "I'll be there in a few minutes. And together sounds wonderful."

Keri winked before she turned away, and he stared at her ass and tatt in happy shock as she returned to the bedside and dressed.

His mate. He'd really and truly found his mate.

He reluctantly stepped into the shower, his wolf sniggering in delight. "Yeah, yeah, you know everything, don't you? Then tell me how I'm going to explain why I'm on this ship in the first place?" he muttered to the beast.

The fiend settled, still smug, as if to say that was a human concern and not his. The wolf had found its mate, and all was right in the world.

6

———————

Her hand shook so hard she was afraid the heavy jeweled brooch resting on her palm would once again end up on the floor. Keri curled her fingers over the surface until the gems spiked into her flesh.

Heaven and hell, that's what the past hour had brought. Getting to finally be with her mate had turned her inside out with happiness. The sex was fabulous, and his confession about his missing sense of smell made the previously confusing situations understandable.

Only when she'd rolled to pick up the dislodged tool belt and discovered the brooch lying on the floor, her heart had not just fallen but shriveled and rolled under the bed, alongside the hastily shoved jewelry.

Mates were chosen by their wolf side. They should be exactly what the other needed, but...she needed a thief?

The evidence lay there, unmistakable and real.

She wanted to scream. In agony, in confusion, in sorrow. Maybe he had a good reason, but wasn't that going to be one of the toughest conversations ever? "You know how you said you couldn't smell? Cool with me. But do you have some financial issues? Are you part of a gang? What's up in your world and will we have to have relationships on visiting days after you're caught and booked for grand theft?"

She was supposed to be acting as a troubleshooter—oh my, there was an issue as well. What was she going to tell Tessa? *Hey, no worries, I've found the thief. But you can't arrest him.*

There had to be a way to solve this that didn't end up involving conjugal visits at the pen every other week.

She tucked the jewel into her desk drawer and got a drink of water. There was time to think. He'd join her, they would visit and she'd manage to get out of him the whys of his situation. Together they would solve this problem.

But first? A little advance chaos control on his behalf.

Tessa answered on the first ring. "Dudette. It's your dime, spill it."

Keri snorted in spite of her worries. "Lay off the Diet Coke, babe."

"Shoot, you think?" A steady *squeak, squeak, squeak* echoed in the background. "Fine. But if you tell me I have to stop the chocolate, there will be a serious discussion happening between my nails and your body."

"Oh, hell no, I'm not getting between a cat and her chocolate."

"What's shaking? Other than your tail?"

"Har har." One small step, that's all she could take right now. And the most important thing was to deal with her suspicions quickly and quietly.

The fact that she needed to roll her mate into bed and crawl all over him a dozen more times before she was anywhere near sated was another matter altogether.

"Tessa—if you don't mind, I'm taking the rest of the day and hiding out."

Squeak, squeak, squeak. "Something wrong? You feeling okay?"

The buzz of need between her legs said one thing. Keri forced her mouth to say another. "I'm fine but need a bit of time away from the crowds. I'll be back in the swing with you tomorrow. Deal?"

"Sure thing. You... Hey, you want me to tell Chad you're not well or something? He stopped in here again a few minutes ago and was asking where you were." *Squeak, squeak, squawk.*

Chad. Gag. "Is he the reason you're doing double-time on the rebounder?"

"Yip. He's like this stick in my side with his constant checking up on me. I'm pretty sure he was never this anal with my brother. Oh, Keri, why can't I be a normal girl and drool over my big brother's friends? Instead, Chad makes my nose itch, and I'm so damn tempted to throw balls every time he comes near to see if he twitches with the urge to play fetch."

The image of ultra-cool Chad clutching a ball in his mouth and sitting at attention made Keri laugh out loud. "Hate to tell you, you are normal. Chad is not your type. Mainly because he is being annoying."

"You were planning on doing him earlier. I take it that plan has changed?"

Like whoa. "I've discovered other interests."

"Oh, really?" The squeaking came to a dead stop, and Keri swore softly at even giving the smallest of openings to the cat's curiosity. Tessa could dig and dig and dig given half a chance. "Keri—what are you doing? Or should I ask, who are you doing?"

Nope. Not going there. "I'll see you in the morning."

"That's not a denial." Happy giggles rose on the other

end of the line. "I expect a full report, because if I'm not getting any action I need to live vicariously through your sexual exploits."

"You've got a whole ship full of willing shifters. Go find your own toy to play with."

Tessa sighed, long and dramatic. "I can't. Gotta be responsible and all that. So you're under full orders to have a big enough blast for us both."

"Thanks. Can I go now, or do you have further plans to make me spill deets?"

"There are already deets?"

Oops. "I'm hanging up now. Bye."

Keri clicked off before she could do any more damage, but at least she'd accomplished her goal. She had the afternoon and evening to spend not only sating her body with her mate but hopefully finding out how to direct the disasterous situation somewhere manageable.

Although the lust clouding her mind would probably distract her for a few hours first.

JARED SHOWERED and dressed in three minutes flat and was hard on Keri's heels. Her determined expression worried him a lot. She was up to something.

Even the concern he felt made him happy though. It was a brand-new sensation, like she was under his skin and he had to help her. He skittered around a corner and flailed his arms backward to avoid slamming into a couple.

"Excuse me." He tucked against the wall to allow them to pass, a man in an extremely sharp business suit and a woman in a dress that screamed expensive. Both of them looked vaguely familiar, and recognition hit in a rush.

Oh hell.

The delighted gasp from the woman made him straighten up and put on his best smile in spite of the pit of despair opening at his feet.

The gasp progressed to a laugh of delight. "How marvelous. Duncan, look who is here. It's Jared Gilliland."

"Whatever are you doing, young man?" A firm finger pressed to the front of his T-shirt as the gentleman stared over his elegant thin-framed glasses. "Traveling a touch on the casual side, aren't you?"

Jared took in the Fedoras with a growing sense of dread. There was no way out of this, no way at all. "Yes, sir. Just a bit of a holiday, and there didn't seem to be a need to dress up. How are you?"

They responded politely while Jared scrambled to find a way to deflect the situation. A trickle of memory hit before they could ask any more awkward questions about his presence on the ship. "My parents mentioned you were looking at some property in the south of France. How did that turn out?"

Distraction was the correct response. They both beamed and described the small resort to him. "Small" meaning there was probably only a legion of staff waiting on the few family members who would visit the premises.

He had spent his entire life working to avoid this situation. Being around the elite wasn't a horrible thing, it just wasn't his thing. His parents had allowed him to step out in his own direction instead of remaining in the limelight of the upper class—which had kept his handicap concealed.

And now? Trapped in a hallway with the leaders of the European werewolves? Way to stay undercover...

Mr. Fedora looked him up and down again, his gaze

narrowing slightly. "Why haven't I seen you in the dining hall? Not once during the entire voyage."

Two pairs of eyes stared into him and Jared wiggled. He hoped he wouldn't get asked a direct question that he didn't want to answer. But then again, if he started down one route then changed tracks, that would be worse. In tough situations there was only one thing to do—tell the truth and hope like hell the dust landed in the right places.

"I slipped on board with nothing but the clothes on my back and I've been doing hard labour ever since because no one knows who I am and I really don't want to tell anyone and I just met my mate and—"

A long, low squeal of delight escaped Mrs. Fedora as she snatched up his hands in her fingers. "Your mate! How simply delightful. You must introduce us."

"Darling. Did you not catch the part where he's traveling incognito? I doubt he wants to trounce down the hallways and have it generally blasted about that he's here. Although I do agree we should help celebrate."

Jared yanked his mouth shut. The adrenaline rush that had started right around the time he'd scented Keri hadn't slowed, and he vibrated like a kite in a high wind. "Right. Secret. Besides, I haven't had a chance to inform my parents, and while I'm honoured, and Keri will be as well, I would appreciate a little longer to make all the announcements I need to take care of."

"We can do secrets. I love secrets."

Oh goodie. Mrs. Fedora was way too into this. "Maybe once the cruise is over—"

"I know!" She clapped her hands with delight. "We can invite you to dinner with us, only as a random seatmate. You know there have been empty seats at the table a few times. That lovely coordinator said we were always welcome to have guests. I'll contact Tessa and you'll get an invitation. I'll tell her we met you during some..." She paused and frowned most adoringly. "What are you doing on board, again?"

Jared blinked in shock at how fast this train was moving on him. "I'm working as an...assistant. General maintenance duties." Nondescript, that was the way to go. Although he was pretty sure that his idiosyncrasies and his parents were fairly well known by this point.

Mr. Fedora wasn't buying it, he could tell. The long aristocratic brow had risen in the air, and Jared resorted to the last-case ammunition he could think of.

"I would love to join you for dinner, only it needs to be in disguise. Please? Because while shifters are usually not the media hounds humans are, I would hate to have your holiday ruined by someone getting the wrong idea and deciding that seeing all of us together is some kind of upcoming international coup."

The most powerful Alpha wolf in England laughed softly. "Up to your old high jinks, are you, Jared? Causing trouble, capturing all the girls' hearts like your father told us about?"

"Not anymore, sir, not now that I have a mate." Even saying the words gave Jared a thrill that cut though the panic in his soul. "But if you issued the invitation to Mark Weaver, and said I was a crew member you'd just met, I would very much appreciate it."

A little more teasing followed before Jared managed to escape with a promise that they would issue the invitation to the dining table in Mark's name. He watched his family friends walk away, the security duo following them a discreet distance behind, but still visible.

He blew out a long breath. Great. The list of troubles

got longer. Now he had an upset mate and royalty to deal with. Not to mention he had to get on the phone to his parents ASAP, because if the news arrived that he'd found his mate before he announced it to them, there would be hell to pay.

Jared raced down the hall toward Keri's room and wondered when he was going to get a chance to stop running and start relaxing. He stood outside and waited, hand hovering over the door. Hesitating to face the music.

In spite of his lack of smell, he knew she was on the other side. And more than that, she was upset about something, and he was dying inside because of it. He changed his mind and thrust the door open, pulling another gasp from her as Keri twirled in surprise to face him.

"You've got to stop scaring me like that," she complained.

In spite of or maybe because of the tension, Jared thought that was just about the funniest thing he'd heard all day. "How do you want me to scare you?"

She snorted, he laughed and some of the tension melted away.

She stepped into his arms and laid her head on his chest. *"I can't believe you're here."*

"I can't believe you didn't smack me over the head sooner." He stroked the damp strands of her hair into order over her shoulders. She'd pulled on a soft blouse that felt like brushed velvet under his fingers, but her hair and skin were softer still. *"I'm glad we found each other."*

"Me too."

Keri pressed her lips to his neck, and he grasped her wrists in his hands to stop himself from crowding closer. "We need to talk, and I already want to eat you alive. No touching or doing anything that could be construed as sexually enticing."

It was a losing proposition. The way she nodded so earnestly at him, her lips pulling into a pout—God, he wanted to drop her to the floor and go all night.

Later later later, his mind reminded.

Soon soon soon, his body blasted back.

She let go and led him to the sitting area in the corner.

"You do have a lot more room than I do. Tell me what your job is on the ship again?" All his good intentions to keep this platonic and nonsexual were vanishing rapidly. He couldn't stay away and linked their fingers together as she talked about Tessa and being friends. When her stream of information slowed to nothing, he braced himself. She batted her lashes. "And you? You had something you need to tell me?"

Just the way she said it made him shiver. As if she already knew those few things he'd neglected to mention, and she was only humouring him and letting him share. "Is this part of a freaky mate thing? Like, I'm never going to be able to have any secrets from you?"

The way she paused increased that eerie sense of other awareness. Then she lifted her gaze and stared into his eyes with this all-knowing look. "I think you can have secrets, but I'll know you have them. Which means you may as well just give in and tell me everything. Because then? We'll be together in whatever we're doing."

Jared sighed. Damn it. Great way to start a forever relationship, based on him being a fool. Excuses spilled out. "I didn't mean anything bad by it."

Her fingers tightened around his, eyes sympathetic. "Sometimes things happen we don't intend."

Relief edged up slightly as he considered he'd avoided

the terrible possibility of her going ballistic at his deception. It looked as if she was going to understand. "They do. It's like one thing leads to another, then another and before I knew it, poof, I was on the ship and I had no idea how to deal with the situation."

Keri nodded slowly, but didn't speak.

Blast. He wished she could actually read his mind. It would be easier than confessing. The upside of getting this over with now? He wouldn't have to listen to her call him by the wrong name during sex again, because that had really given him the skeevies.

"I'm not Mark."

The solid eye contact remained, but the understanding smile pasted on her face faded a little. Her lips twitched. "What?"

Okay, as a confession, let alone an explanation, that one really had sucked. Jared wrinkled his nose and tried again.

"When I came on this ship and said I was Mark? I lied. I was—" Oh man, good thing she was a shifter and should be cool about the sex thing, but still... Telling her he'd gone from having someone else in his bed to her? Dangerous territory. He swallowed hard and spat out the rest in a rush. "I was running away from a lover's family and the ship seemed a good place to hide. Then Chad cornered me and I said yes, I was Mark, and—"

"You're telling me your big confession is you're not one of the officially hired staff?" She wiggled back, the furrow between her brows deepening.

Silence echoed.

"Umm, yeah?"

"That's *it*?"

Jared rocked for a moment. The unexpected disappointment in her voice was more than a little confusing. "That's not enough? I've been impersonating one of my pack mates. I think he might have been drunk and..."

He stuttered to a stop. She had one brow raised so high he was worried she'd get a cramp. Jared slid his hands around her torso and tugged her into his lap. He buried his face against her neck and breathed deeply. Only the faintest of scents reached him, but with her taste still fresh in his mind, and this really cool sensation tickling the back of his spine—the sense of her—he was surrounded and content even though they had so much more to figure out.

He squeezed her until the tension eased, her shoulders softening, body easing against him. Her breathing picked up and his body reacted to every little nuance.

When he turned his head toward hers, their lips met. Slow, easy, then more and more needy. It was no use. The draw of their wolves was too much to ignore, and further discussions would have to be put aside for a while. He took her down to the mattress and settled in for an extended lovemaking session.

7

———

Keri sprawled on her back, one foot hanging off the edge of the bed. She'd dragged a pillow over her face to stop the light sneaking in the small portside window from shining into her eyes.

Thoroughly satisfied. Boneless relaxation. She considered rolling over and looking around the room, but she didn't have the energy to even do that.

Mark, no, *Jared*—her mate—had started with a slow seduction of her body that had gone on for hours. Speeding up, slowing down. They'd basically covered the entire room and the bath before the last time when she'd buried her teeth in his neck to stop from screaming during her orgasm.

There was no doubt about the physical connection between them. Maybe a couple of wolves farther up the hierarchy would have been able to hold off their animal sides to get to the bottom of the talking they had to do. For them, both firmly mired in the middle of the pack? Their wolves were stronger than the human side when they wanted something, and they'd both wanted their mates, badly.

She wiggled her fingers across the mattress in search of his warm body. Her inner beast stirred with more curiosity than lust, and Keri was both happy and sad. It wasn't every day a girl got mated, but they really should do something other than burn up the sheets. It would be good if the animal side allowed them to take a short breather.

Her hand found nothing—not even a warm patch on the empty sheets—and she shoved the pillow away from her face as she rolled sideways and searched the room.

There was a note lying beside her and she grabbed it, collapsing back as her stomach muscles protested. Hmm, that bit of reverse cowboy had worn her out more than she thought.

She lifted both hands in the air and stared skyward at the writing. His letters were strong and bold and definitely masculine.

Hmm, masculine.

She beat down her inner husky to concentrate on the words.

Hi lover.

My phone went off while you were still sleeping like an angel, so I went to grab a few things. We've been invited to dinner. Kind of have to go—I'll explain later, but in the meantime, rest up. We've got a lot to talk about.

You look delicious asleep, BTW.

Jared

Keri padded to the bathroom to soak her head and get fully awake. The clock over the dresser said it was five p.m. already, and the first dinner settings were at six.

A dinner invitation they had to meet? Her confusion returned fourfold. She really hoped this had nothing to do with the stolen jewelry. Oh God, she couldn't stand to have just met him and have him taken away.

All kinds of scenarios raced through her mind. Him being blackmailed to steal. Him as the linchpin of a shifter mob who infiltrated shifter-only events and...

"Arghhhhh." She rubbed her hair in an attempt to rid herself of the circular logic racing through her brain.

The towel covering her head must have masked the noise of the door because the next thing she knew there was a set of gentle hands assisting in drying her long hair. Jared slipped the towel away, and the light shone on his strong jaw and gorgeous brown eyes.

"Hey. You okay?"

Those eyes—those couldn't be the eyes of a criminal. It would be such a rotten shame. Instinctively she stepped against his body and accepted his embrace. Not a word until the opportune moment. "Hey yourself. Light sleeper?"

"Only when there's this really hot woman cuddled up to me so tight I'm unable to breathe she's turning me on so hard."

The tension in Keri's belly wiggled off the cool setting onto the burner set to high, and she whimpered in pain. "Not fair. Your note said eating, not crawling all over each other for another four hours."

His hand cupped her face, thumb gentle over her bottom lip. "It is rather bad timing, isn't it? Can't be helped. We'll have to work together to convince our wolves to act politely for a couple hours while we dine, and then I promise we can come back here and continue until you can't stand me bringing you to another climax."

Another whimper escaped as she pictured returning to the room. "We need to change the topic. This isn't helping."

He brushed his lips over hers, stealing a kiss before stepping back and nodding solemnly. "Distraction needed. I agree."

The cards he held forward caught her attention, all right. Official cruise seating-arrangement cards for the first-class dining hall. Shifters had hierarchies on top of hierarchies. The average pack might be very relaxed about some things, like sex, but you didn't cross a line uninvited, and money and power often went hand in hand.

"Jared? Where did you get those?"

"I told you we had invites for dinner." He looked away for a brief moment then returned to meet her gaze with a smile. "One of the upper-class families had room at their table, and I heard they've been inviting people to join them —kind of a *be nice to the masses* gesture, I guess."

Keri opened the gold-gilded card with shaking fingers. There was her name written in fancy-schmancy script, seven o'clock seating time and the Fedoras' official crest pressed into the wax seal.

Oh. Boy.

Sheer willpower kept her gaze connected with his. What she wanted to do was glance at the drawer where she'd tucked the brooch—the costs-some-ungodly-amount brooch she was pretty sure belonged to the Fedoras. But giving away the fact she knew something was up wouldn't solve the problem.

Sudden raw anxiety wrapped around her like a miniature tornado.

It was annoying that the first thing that really caused her to panic had nothing to do with the thefts.

"I don't have a thing—"

"—to wear?" His smile flashed instantly and he looked almost proud. "If you'll allow me to solve that issue, I picked us up a couple things at the shop. They had your size on file from the staff list. Please, don't say no. It's my...mating gift to you."

He'd pointed to the right, and for the first time she noticed the hangers hooked over the wall sconce. Something dark hung against the wall—a suit jacket, perhaps. But in front there was a shimmering red gown that made her gasp in surprise and dismay.

"Oh, Jared. How did you—?"

He caught her against him and kissed her protests away. It was a touch annoying, and yet how could she object when his mouth was doing such sinfully distracting things?

He drew away slowly, as if gauging to see if the complaints would pour out again. "I want you to feel comfortable tonight. I know it's just a dress-up-to-dress-up thing. But you are so beautiful, I had to get you something that was nearly as pretty as you."

"Silver-tongued devil..." Keri smiled slowly. It wasn't her jeans and ratty T-shirts, but she wasn't into being a rebel for rebellion's sake anymore—she'd gotten over that as a teenager. He placed a hand on her lower back, directing her toward the clothing. The heat of his palm lingered against her flesh.

Contradictions raged inside, an emotional and mental battleground. She slid the back of her fingers down the material, a shiver racing over her at the sheer decadence of the fabric. She loved being cared for—and wearing this dress would make some of her little-girl daydreams come true. She was a princess being cared for by her fairy godmother.

Said *godmother* pressed against her back, and the image switched from pumpkins and formal balls to Little Red Riding Hood and the Big Bad Wolf, who was now nibbling on her neck and the sensitive place behind her ear.

Big Bad Wolf was a better image to keep in mind than some kind and helpless old matriarch.

But the invitation had been issued. Declining would be

massively rude, i.e., rude enough to be mentioned, and suddenly Tessa's reputation was on the line and Keri was ready to laugh out loud.

It was easy to justify what you wanted to do in the first place, wasn't it? She let her other protests die away for a moment as she turned to face him. "It's simply incredible. Thank you."

The expression lighting his eyes made her incredibly happy right before a tiny corner of guilt snuck in. Had the gown been paid for with stolen funds?

Screw it. She couldn't hide in the sand like an ostrich forever, but for the next three hours? She would take the pretense of the fairy tale and roll with it. Keep her eyes wide open and hope her heart wasn't about to be broken into pieces.

JARED COAXED the smile back to Keri's face, and finally his wolf stopped slapping him around. The beast hadn't stopped *poke, poke, poking* since he'd hit the damn ship. He'd figured it was because of the mate thing, but now that he and Keri had gotten together—and wow, nothing had prepared him for how much better sex with a mate was— Jared had figured his wolf would take a chill pill.

Nope. Still with the *poke-poke* shit. The stupid beast sensed something was wrong with his mate and wanted to fix it, right *now*. Jared couldn't figure out what the lupine was going on about, which made both of them slightly pissed off and started the typical shifter internal-domination games.

Two-brains-in-one-head couldn't always live together in harmony, and this was one of those times.

Keri had pulled the gown off the wall and was flipping the hanger back and forth, checking both sides. He could hardly wait to see her in it. The skimpy garment had a low, low back, which should showcase that incredible tattoo she had. Which was a good thing.

The scoop of the fabric also meant that when he managed to sweet-talk her into dancing after dinner, he'd get to have his hand on bare flesh. Which was also a good thing.

There was no way she could wear a bra with that neckline. A very, very good thing.

He was such a dog.

"Oh!" Jared fumbled in his pocket. "I checked. If you want, you can get your hair done. And your...whatever else you want. They can sneak you in so you're ready in time for our seating."

Keri took the salon's card from him and that brow of hers went up again. "You think I need a haircut?"

Jared stopped in confusion. That wasn't the response he'd expected. "Umm, no, but I thought you might enjoy getting done up all fancy."

The pause was barely there, but he still noticed. He'd made her uncomfortable, and that was the last thing he'd intended. His wolf gave him shit and this time he agreed.

"Actually, I stopped at the salon to grab a bottle of massage oil so I can seduce the crap out of you later, and then I thought most women love to be pampered and stuff." Jared grabbed her hands and squeezed them tightly. Starting a lifetime relationship not knowing a thing about the other person was freaking hard, but damn if he'd mess it up over something as inconsequential as a dinner out. "That whole 'I'm yours, you're mine' thing? I meant it. In everything, even in the little things. Hell, especially in the little things that make you happy. If you tell me you want to go to dinner in our jeans, I'm game. I don't mind pushing the boundaries of politeness, but I also want to give you special things. You can dye your hair neon green and I'll still think you are gorgeous. You can—"

It was his turn to be kissed into silence. Keri all but crawled up him, and her tongue was down his throat, and if he didn't exercise more control than he wanted to, he was going to be buried in her body and not let either of them come up for air all night long.

It took every ounce of strength to catch hold of her hair, wrap it around his fist and tug lightly. She gasped, not with pain, but something sweet and dark and *dammit*, his cock couldn't possibly get any harder, but it did.

"You're going to make us late for dinner."

She grinned. "I'm sorry I misunderstood your offer. I'd love to hit the salon, on one condition."

He knew that look. Oh man, he'd seen it on his mom and sisters when they were about to do a little "improving" on him. "No. Please, no."

She batted her lashes.

"Oh, as if that's fair. Using your physical addictiveness to entice me into a salon? You'd do that to me?"

She stroked her fingers through his hair. "I like how you look as well, Mr. Gilliland, but if we're going to do this, let's do it up right. I doubt we'll be dining with royalty very often in our lifetime. Why not make it a night to remember?"

Jared grinned. "Deal."

Keri shuffled past him. He called to confirm their bookings as he watched her pull on minuscule underwear. It wasn't the right moment to expand on the fact this was probably going to be the first of many such dinners.

He didn't want to freak her out too badly.

"Thirty seconds and I'll be ready."

Jared waved as she disappeared into the bathroom. He leaned back on the desk then remembered he'd better phone his parents before the night was over, but the call was bound to take more time than he currently had. If he forgot, and his folks heard from someone else, his ass would be in a sling. Only, what were the odds he'd be too distracted when they returned to her room?

Better safe than sorry. He slipped open the drawer looking for a piece of paper to leave himself a reminder. He'd plop it in the middle of the bed so they couldn't miss it.

Jackpot. A notepad.

He grasped a page, tugging to remove it from the pad, and the entire drawer jerked forward. Displaying a very familiar diamond-and-ruby pendant tucked into the back corner.

"Keri—?" Panic sealed his lips in mid-question.

Oh shit. Oh *shit*. Jared darted a glance toward the bathroom to make sure the door was still closed, then palmed the brooch and slipped it into his pocket.

His heart pounded as if he'd been racing around the deck whilst being chased by some of the bigger and nastier cougar shifters, the type who were known to provide loans with horrible interest rates to the losers hanging out in the onboard casino.

Not that he'd had any business with those kind of riffraff, but they were a part of shifter culture as much as human society.

The brooch rested in his pocket like a lump of coal, ready to burn his life to ashes. It wasn't fair, but then, life wasn't fair. He was old enough to know that truth.

Keri stepped from the bathroom and joined him with a happy smile. "Ready to go."

He put his best face forward. "We've got plenty of time. We'll come back to change if that's okay."

She wrapped her fingers around his arm and they stepped together up the hallway.

They were quiet as they strode the hall. Jared was too busy thinking about what the hell he was going to do to solve this shit of a mess to make polite conversation.

Keri cleared her throat. "It's weird, isn't it? This whole mate thing?"

The question helped him focus, the innocent query deceptively complex. It was as if she were completely a part of him and yet completely hidden behind a wall. "I can sense little things I didn't expect. And I like your sense of humour. I know a lot of people who have found their mates, and they've always told me that the relationship was totally right, just what they'd been looking for."

Keri stumbled a little, and he braced her. "You okay?"

She nodded then blurted out, "Am I what you've been looking for?"

The brooch slowed his step, a ball and chain of worry weighing him down.

Her fingers tightened before he could respond. "Jared? You okay? I...I'm sorry if I put you on the spot. Let me say that differently. I *hope* I can become what you've always wanted in a mate."

And with those brave words, all his fears vanished. He turned her into his arms and rested his forehead against hers. Taking slow breaths, looking into her eyes and seeing her soul.

Finding out his mate was possibly the thief everyone was talking about belowdecks had momentarily freaked him out. But she was right—people could change. He was going to support her every way he could, and they could move forward into a new life together.

"I know it's early, and we don't know each other completely yet, but Keri, I'm going to fall in love with you. Thoroughly and completely. So you'd better bet you're what I've always wanted in a mate."

A tiny crease marred the corners of her eyes as she fought back tears. *"We can do this, can't we? We can fall in love, as well as our wolves?"*

"Oh yes." Jared pushed his wolf as far into the corner as he could. For once the beast went with only a second's *pfft* at being told to bugger off. *"We're going to fall in love so hard our wolves are going to be jealous of our human sides."*

Keri laughed out loud. "Yeah, right."

Jared kissed her laughing lips, her mouth still open as he captured her. It was a short exchange, with more tenderness than passion. A kiss of hopeful need and yearning to belong mixed with promises of long days and years to come.

Jared would make sure they fell in love.

But first, he had to find some way to return the brooch to the Fedoras without Keri being caught. Because the distinctive arrangement was most definitely his father's handiwork, and had been a family gift to the rulers a few years back.

8

____

"**S**hut. Up." Tessa wasn't bouncing, she was staring, slack-jawed, as Keri attempted to tug her hand free from Jared's firm grasp. "You are the special guests dining with the Fedoras? And who'd you steal the dress from?"

"It's a long story. Really, very boring. You don't want to know the details at all because they'd literally make you tip over and fall asleep."

Tessa waved a dismissive hand in front of Keri's face and stepped closer to Jared, eyeing him down, then up, then down again. Jared all cleaned up and dressed in a formal suit was enough to make any woman's knees weak. "Well, _well_. When my friend goes hunting, she finds lovely prey."

How Jared managed to keep a straight face, Keri wasn't sure. "You have such a way of setting everyone at ease. You must work as the cruise director or something."

"Just saying." Tessa dipped her chin politely at Jared a second before Keri suspected she was going to jump him. "When you decide you're tired of him, I'd be happy to take him off—"

Keri's wolf growled.

Tessa's eyes shot wide open even as she stepped back in defense, the cat grin breaking free.

"Oh my, there's more to this story than a shipboard fling, isn't there?" Tessa swung a finger between the two of them before leaning forward slightly to whisper conspiratorially. "You guys got that doggies-in-love-forever thing happening, don't you?"

Jared bowed formally. "You are the soul of discretion, I can see. Yes, we're mates, and I'm very happy to have found Keri. You'll have to tell me all about your college days some time."

Keri wondered that Jared could small talk so easily. Although the charm-the-panties-off-the-women bit he'd shared about? Was an ix-nay orever-fay from this point on. "Personally, I'm all for stringing her into a corner and hanging catnip about a foot out of reach. You're being far too nice to her."

"Your friends are my friends, right?"

Yeah, sort of. Unless that meant he was going to introduce her to the mafia and expect her to accept them as well. A little of the glow of happiness left the moment.

She turned to Tessa, who now wore this shit-eating grin. "Stop that."

"What?"

"You know."

Tessa snorted. "I'm thinking about all those stories you told me during college, and how much you'll pay me now to not reveal your secrets."

"She's a feisty one, isn't she?" Jared asked.

"BFF. Means I love her to pieces but occasionally want to throttle her."

"Understandable."

Jared tugged Keri closer to his side. "Sorry, Tessa, but I need to steal Keri away. We'll talk to you soon, but we don't want to be late for our dinner date." He dipped his head politely, the crisp cut of his suit almost squeaking as he moved.

Tessa sighed and wiggled her fingers. "You all have fun. Unlike some people, who have work to do."

The walk across the thick plushy carpet felt different today, and not just because they were headed to a meeting with a couple so far above her current position Keri was afraid she'd get a nosebleed. It was the glittering lights of the formal chandeliers overhead. It was the silky slide of the fabric over her bare skin—Jared had convinced her she should leave off the undies along with her bra to avoid having panty lines. But most of all, it was her mate walking beside her, his elbow bumping her lightly as she clung to his arm, his fingers folded over hers. How he managed to look as if that suit was his normal everyday wear impressed her and scared her to death.

She'd either mated one of the world's most instinctively talented actors or...or... she had no idea what was going on.

"You okay?" Jared pulled her to a stop outside the first-class formal dining room. *"If there's something wrong, please... We don't have to do this. I can make our excuses—"*

"No." As much as she wanted to. "But thank you for asking."

Enough mental chaos. She'd been on a damn roller coaster all day. But their conversation before hitting the salon—it was true. They could fall in love, they could make this work for their human sides and their animals.

Enjoy this moment then deal with the rest.

She kissed his cheek and stepped forward with him, shoulders squared, spine tall. And if there were butterflies still tangoing in her belly? Well, maybe they wanted to have a little dancing time as well.

~

JARED WAS IMPRESSED. More than impressed—it was once again made crystal clear why the Fedoras were in the position they were.

Power as a wolf was easy to define. Charisma was harder. While a strong wolf could order you around, it took a special kind of personality to have people ignore your power and trust you and want to please you in spite of your strength.

Mr. Fedora had charmed and eased Keri through the entire meal. From the moment he'd risen and pulled out her chair, there had been light chitchat and easy conversation. No mention of anything that could be considered off topic— like their recent mating, even though that had to be all too obvious to anyone with a nose, other than himself. Mrs. Fedora had been equally attentive, and dinner had flown past.

He wondered why he'd spent so much time away from society when there were such good people there. Although —thinking back to the coffee shop and all the leaders of the Granite Lake pack—his friends might be a little rougher around the edges, but they too were awesome people to spend time with.

The music picked up and Jared rose to his feet as Mr. Fedora did.

"I am going to dance with my wife, but first?" Fedora turned to Keri and offered her a hand. "Might I take a turn with you, young lady?"

Keri's cheeks flushed. Her gaze darted to meet Jared's

and that alone filled him with pride. Not like she had to ask permission, but that she wanted to check with him, and the resulting wash of connection between them? Man, this mate thing was very, very cool.

"*I am so jumping you later...*" he promised, grinning as her face turned bright red.

He turned to Mrs. Fedora and offered a hand, and the four of them stepped onto the polished boards of the empty dance area.

Mrs. Fedora wasted no time. "She's a simply lovely creature. I approve."

Jared chuckled. "Thanks."

Her smile widened. "You puppies are all the same. Yes, dear, I know I don't have any say in it, but I still approve. Your mother is going to love her. Keri's got that little bit of steel in her spine that will make it easier for her to handle the media when they get a hold of you." She paused then stared him in the eyes. "You will have to have a formal party at some point. I mean, I understand your wolf sides are already happily together, but there is certain decorum to follow."

He nodded, turning her smoothly even as he kept an eye on Keri, hoping she was all right. "I know, but give me the time to explain everything to Keri. It's not that unusual a situation—mates meeting out of the blue happens all the time, but I doubt she expected me and the accompanying chaos my family will bring."

"But your wolves understand. She can handle it." Mrs. Fedora's expressive face changed. "You have, in your slightly unorthodox manner, been hiding out from the world. Perhaps it's time for that to come to an end."

"Don't blame me—Mom and Dad were the ones who chose Alaska to move to. And it's not hiding out, not really."

The elegant brow went up again. "Okay, it's hiding out a little, but it worked. We've been happy as a family out of the spotlight."

She tilted her head and fell silent, and he realized the interrogation was over.

If only the brooch burning a hole in his pocket was back in her possession. He spun his partner to check out the dance floor. Keri was still smiling, a happy kind of overwhelmed-but-in-a-good-way sensation sneaking his direction. There were more dancers now, surrounding them as they spun and twirled.

Perfect distraction. He reached into his pocket to grab the jewel, then replaced his hand on Mrs. Fedora's waist quickly. It was only a second later he realized his idea of pinning the jewels to her and having her "find" them was a bad idea. She'd never be stupid enough to believe she'd sat through an entire meal without noticing.

Frustrated, he brought his hand back and dropped the brooch into his pocket.

~

KERI STUMBLED, and Mr. Fedora caught her beautifully. "Everything all right, my dear?"

She nodded quickly and propped up her smile, the corners feeling a little shaky. She'd just seen her mate remove a jewel from Mrs. Fedora's dress and pocket it. All her hopeful wishes about the thievery being a misunderstanding fled.

She had to save him from himself. "It's been lovely, but could I dance with my mate?"

Sheer elegance poured from the man as he tilted his head and smoothly brought them over to the other couple.

A moment later Keri was in Jared's arms, physical need rising and frustration not far behind.

"Are you having a good time?" he asked.

"It's been incredible."

Jared nodded and pulled her closer as the music slowed. She took total advantage and snuck her hand into his pocket, palming the stolen goods and bringing it out to hide it...

Shit. Hide it where? There was nothing but a thin layer of fabric covering her entire body, and unless she wanted to be doing weird body-cavity stuff, no way could she keep it around for long. She carefully rested her hand on his shoulder, thumb tucked in to hold the jewel, her palm completely covering it.

Under the table she spotted two purses, and really bad inspiration hit. She had to return the jewel to the other woman's purse and everything would be fine.

Jared nuzzled the side of her neck lightly and she shivered.

Damn wolf hormones, cruise ships and diamonds. All of them, just damn, damn, *damn*.

Jared savoured the sensation of Keri all tight up against him, the knowledge that he was only millimeters away from her naked skin settling and riling up his wolf simultaneously. He adjusted position and two things happened. First he caught a tiny flash of dazzling light from under her fingers. Then a quick pat of his pocket revealed it was empty. All his hopes that she wasn't really the thief vanished, and he struggled to hide his sadness.

It was no use. She stiffened, probably sensing his upset. *"What's wrong?"*

He didn't answer. Under the table he'd spotted two purses. If he could just get the jewel back in Mrs. Fedora's, they could have the next part of the conversation in private. *"Nothing will be wrong, but I need it back."*

He spun her gently, giving her time to tighten her grip around what he assumed was the brooch. She swirled out, then back, and he twisted them together, her back tight to his front. He caught her fingers in his and slid both their hands into his jacket pocket.

"Drop it," he ordered. Keri resisted for a second, but she had to realize if she waited too long all eyes would be on them. *"Now, please."*

Her fingers opened and they moved on, sliding apart in the dance. He kept a firm grip on her other wrist so she couldn't escape. They came back together and he brought their torsos close to make sure she was trapped.

"Oh, Jared, why?"

Even in his head her frustration was crystal clear. *"It's got to be done."*

"Please let me have it, and I promise—"

"It's okay, I've got everything under control. We can talk about the details later. Just know that I will not let anyone arrest you. You're going to be fine. Trust me." He put all his caring into the thoughts, all his growing love, because as bizarre as this chaos was, he was falling in love and nothing could stop him from protecting his mate.

The tension in her body changed. *"What do you mean, I won't be arrested?"*

The music slowed and they all stood to applaud the band for a moment before he offered his arm to lead her back to their table. He was still eyeing the purses and trying to figure the best way to get at the one he needed. *"I mean it. If the brooch is returned there's no reason for any arrests. I can... Well, I have connections."*

Keri sat prettily even as bewilderment poured off her. *"This is so confusing. Why would I be arrested for trying to return a jewel that you stole?"*

9

They didn't say a word beyond polite conversation as they made their excuses and left the ballroom. Keri kept hold of his elbow, stopping him outside one of the formal boardrooms and stabbing in the access code before all but shoving him into the space. She didn't bother to flick on additional switches, leaving them in the low security lighting that cast shadows and lent a mysterious air to the room.

The beautiful panorama outside the full line of windows overlooking the glittering Pacific Ocean, along with the lights shining off the passing islands, was seen and discarded in a second flat.

He leaned a hip on the massive oak board table, looking all hunky and tasty and stuff, and she had to reel in her hormones big time.

She was pissed off—an important detail to remember—but in the face of six feet of delicious mate, it was really, really difficult.

Then he reached into his pocket, pulled out the brooch and laid it on the table beside him. Even in the low lighting the thing sparkled enough that if Tessa would have been here? She'd have been batting it around in an instant.

Keri pointed. "That. That's not yours."

He coughed briefly. "Well, strictly speaking, it is, but it isn't."

"Arghhhh!" She stomped across the room, gripped his elegant lapels and got right in his face. "That brooch has been reported missing or stolen. I'm trying to save your ass here, mate, so enough with the cryptic responses. Why did I find it in your tool belt?"

Instant confusion. "In my tool belt? I found the brooch in your desk drawer and recognized it. I didn't want you to get in trouble so I grabbed it with the intention of—"

"Wait. You found it in my desk? Okay, fine. I totally want to know why you were rummaging around in my desk in the first place, but the brooch was in the drawer *because*..." Keri paused for effect, "...I found it in your tool belt. So there."

Jared continued to shake his head as if confused. She was still right up against his body, the heat between them growing. He wrapped his arms around her almost absentmindedly as he spoke. "But I didn't take it. Honest."

Staring into his eyes there was no way she doubted his sincerity. Okay, maybe a lust-driven, hormonally charged wolf wasn't the best bet for discerning truth, but it was all she had to work with. "Then how did it get into your tool belt?"

They gazed into each other's faces, his fingers trickling over her shoulders again and again as they considered. The constant motion calmed her. Eased her nervous twitching as a million scenarios raced through her brain. Had someone planted it on him? Should they be double-checking the security tapes in the staff room?

It hit at the same moment.

"The bookshelf," they both shouted.

He picked her up and twirled her, and she laughed with relief. "Oh my goodness, I thought you were in all kinds of trouble and I was going to have to sit outside your cell and pass you peanut butter sandwiches or something."

"And I thought you'd gotten into trouble...but that's enough. We both assumed, and we were wrong." He lowered her to the table. Stepped back slightly. "We don't know each other—it's only been a day, really."

Keri nodded, a huge sigh of relief escaping her. She clung to his fingers, refusing to let him escape. "So in the interest of easing your mind. I'm not a thief. I have a degree in modern art—which means I'm usually employed as a barista. Tessa got me this gig on the ship to hold her hand while she's running things for the first time—she's the business-admin-with-honours student. We've been friends for years, and then we roomed together even though she went into a different program than me."

His smile was real. "That's the best kind of friends. People who like you for who you are, and not who you *are...*"

"Totally." She paused as he kissed her, standing between her legs to hold himself tight to her body. He cupped her chin as he stole the air from her lungs.

Much later he kept a tight hold but spoke next to her ear. "I'm not a thief either. I live in Haines, Alaska. Mom and Dad moved there to start their family in a nice quiet location out of the limelight. They and my sisters moved away to another of the family homes a number of years ago, but I decided to stick with the North."

One of the family homes?

Keri pushed him back to see him smiling sheepishly. "Go on."

"Well, the family is kind of in...a good financial position." He nodded more enthusiastically. "So I do work, but I also get to do a lot of volunteering and—"

She wasn't a cat, but this slow trickle of non-information was killing her. "Jared? What are you not telling me? Don't you think not knowing stuff has already caused enough trouble?"

"Definitely, only I don't want to freak you out."

She laughed and clutched his neck, pulling him back in for another brief kiss. "If you're not a thief, I don't think anything you say can freak me out. Just tell me."

"Jewels. The family is into jewels. One of the things I do in the North is travel between the four shops the family owns that are located in resort towns along the cruise-tour route. I also help my dad with sketches for layouts—we work online. That brooch? I recognized it because it was commissioned as a gift. My father and I designed it a couple years ago as a birthday gift for my mom's best friend."

Her heart might have skipped a beat, which was why there was this ringing in her ears causing her to hear things that couldn't possibly have been said.

"Your mom and Mrs. Fedora are...best friends?"

He nodded slowly.

"So...you're not a thief because you could buy that brooch?"

"I could buy this boat."

Change of mindset needed. The rags-to-riches makeover took a few seconds, and the result was she didn't really know what to say.

"Okay."

He leaned over her where she sat on the table. "Okay? That's it?"

"Well, I figured dancing on the table would seem like a bit of a mercenary response. As would screaming *holy shit I hit the jackpot!*"

His laugh deepened. "So glad you're not running away in fear like I'd expected."

"Fear?"

He nodded. "Because that dinner tonight? Was very informal compared to what we've got coming down the line. I can ask my parents to keep the parties small, but there will be a few events we'll have to attend, like a mating party for some family and business friends."

A shiver raced over her skin. Maybe she needed to borrow Tessa's rebounder and sprint for a while. "How many friends are we talking about?"

He shrugged. "Six? Seven?"

She snorted in derision before realizing he couldn't mean only that many people. Her mouth went dry. "Hundred?"

She held her breath in anticipation. The pause was worse than an answer.

Well, not really.

"Thousand."

The pent-up air in her lungs escaped in a gasp and she bolted.

He caught her before she could hit the door and hoisted her over his shoulder. "No, no running away."

Keri laughed and pounded on his back. "Put me down. I'm kidding. I mean, oh my, that's a hell of a lot of people all wanting to sniff us, but as long as you're there, it'll be fine."

Jared lowered her back to the tabletop. "Seriously?"

"Seriously. Poor little me can deal with having mated a millionaire."

"Oh, you found someone else? With less money?"

She smacked him on the shoulder even as they laughed together. Then he rolled with her to the middle of the table and proceeded to remove all thought of thefts, parties and cash of any sort. Her dress went one way, his suit the other, until the only thing left between them was skin.

It had been a hell of a day. A hell of a good day.

10

———

*J*ared stared at his clothes and wondered if swearing like a coal miner in front of his new mate would lose him all the brownie points he'd gained the day before. "Umm, Keri?"

She strolled out of her bathroom in the buff, and he fought to keep from drooling on the carpet. "Yes?"

Concentrate. "You remember I showed up naked yesterday?"

"I don't think I'll ever forget." She pulled open drawers, and he was really distracted when she bent to get something from the bottom drawer, her naked ass facing—

Oh boy. *Concentrate harder.* "A co-worker grabbed my things for me and hung them to dry. Someone was nice enough to drop them off here for me this morning, all folded and everything."

"Well, that is nice."

"No, it's not."

He held the pile out. She slipped a T-shirt over her head before coming to his side. "What's wrong?"

There was a largish bulge in the front of his jeans—well,

he'd had such a thing, but never without actually being *in* the pants before. And when Keri reached into his pocket, the mysterious objects she pulled out and laid on top of the fabric were exactly what he'd thought they'd find.

A fist full of watches, necklaces and shining diamond earrings.

"You have a very classy tailor."

Jared snorted in relief. "You're not mad at me?"

"For what? Good taste in jeans?" Keri patted his naked ass and his blood pressure shot skyward. "That pair with the tatters and the threadbare patch on the crotch you wore when you came on board? Makes me all growly. Especially the part right here..."

His clothes and everything with them fell to the floor as he grabbed her wrist a second after she'd grabbed *his* jewels. She cupped him gently and he swallowed hard. "Someone put that stuff in there to get me in trouble."

"Of course they did. But we'll figure out who."

Jared groaned as she continued to torture him with her touch. "I have to get to work. Keri, love, stop. You're killing me."

She kissed his shoulder and squeezed gently one last time before retreating with a sigh. "Yes, me too. The work bit, as well as the *killing me*. Let me take the pile of contraband to Tessa, and we'll get everything back to the proper places. Don't worry about it."

"Tessa's going to think you've gone nuts."

"She'll understand. She's a shifter—I mean, she's a cat, but she gets the mate thing. And you do have an impeccable record, right?"

"And I could buy the boat?"

"That too..." Keri leapt into his arms, clinging like a limpet. "I know I joked about your financial situation, and

I'm not mad that you have money, but don't think that's the reason you make me happy, okay?"

He kissed her nose, squeezed her tightly. He dressed and sent up a request to whatever shipboard deities there were that time would fly until they could be together again.

Alone. He should have added *alone with Keri* to his request. Because it was only thirty minutes after he'd left Keri to head to what he expected would be a dirty, filthy, miserable job assignment before he saw her again.

And they weren't alone. *Least Likely Chaperone for a thousand, Alex...*

"You nearly done?"

Chad leaned on the wall, arms folded, and got in the way. The man wasn't close enough for Jared to shove the toilet plunger over his face, but the thought was tempting. "It's not working. Looks like we'll need a snake."

"Why don't you go get one?" Chad suggested.

He could do one better. Jared pulled out his phone and texted quickly. "It'll be here in a minute."

Chad frowned. "Really?"

"Really. It's called delegating, Chad. You should try it sometime. I'm here, elbows deep in a project, so one of the guys currently walking the floor will bring the things we need. How long have you been working on this ship, anyway?"

Okay, he wasn't being as polite as he'd been the day before. But knowing the creep had been after Keri made Jared's fur stand on end which, when he was in human form, was a really uncomfortable sensation.

"This is my sixth trip. I did five with Tessa's brother. Now there was a guy who knew how to run things."

Not if he hired you four more times. "Tessa seems to be doing a great job."

"She's a girl."

Jared kept his mouth shut but his brain screamed *good observation, genius.*

Chad didn't need any encouragement. "Always that type. Get the job because they're family, you know. Flash a little hip, and then poof, they've got the position someone more competent should have."

"Really. Were you looking for her position?"

Chad laughed. "Me? Nahhh. I like coordinating behind the scenes. The front-line stuff was Tony's place. He was good at it. Should come back."

Jared wasn't going to waste air responding. The guy clearly wasn't listening to anything but his own voice.

Silence reigned except for the sound of sloshing water as he worked the stopped-up water lines.

Who knew that the summers he'd spent hanging out with the pool staff would have taught him so much about plumbing? Life really was an education.

The door squeaked open behind them, and instant delight hit at seeing Keri step in, followed by a quickly beaten-down urge to kill as Chad peeled himself off the wall and sauntered into her path.

And stopped.

"Holy fuck, you smell like him." Chad pointed to Jared. "You been turning me down to hump a grease jockey?"

Keri planted both hands on her hips and glared. "You're in my way."

"Really, Keri, really?" Chad inched aside but raised his volume. "All this time? You choose that mongrel over me?"

Jared watched intently, just to make sure if Chad did do anything inappropriate, he'd be able to leap from the maintenance hold and rip the ass's head off. And because he was paying close attention, he saw it all, like poetry in motion. Keri timed her step past Chad so her hip connected at the perfect angle to send him sprawling into the open space that was filled with overflow from the stopped up pipes.

Two additional careful steps brought her safely over the piping lining the floor, then she kicked slightly, like a dog covering her business, and Jared clamped his mouth shut to stop from roaring with laughter.

She reached out the loops of metal he needed for the job. The sweet smile on her face let him know she was content to have put Chad in his place all on her own.

"Here you go. I was headed this way, and thought I'd stop by to say hi."

"Hi."

There was dirty water around Jared's feet, a slightly nasty smell in the air, but having Chad on his ass and her mate grinning back at her made the moment pretty damn bright. "I'm not going to kiss you. Not right now."

Jared shook his head. "Save it for later. Having a good day?"

Before she could answer, a growl rose behind Keri. Chad stumbled to his feet, cursing loudly.

Jared leaned to the side. "I imagine the cruise labour relations has rules about that kind of language. I might have to put in a formal complaint if you keep it up."

Chad flicked his fingers and dirty water sprayed everywhere. "You two deserve each other."

He spun and exited the room, his jeans soaking wet.

Keri sighed. "I'm sorry, I guess I shouldn't have done that."

"Well, it's not as if I'm worried I'm going to get fired. He's a jerk. Don't worry about him."

She nodded as she found a dry spot on top of one of the mechanical boxes. "Still, unless you're going to..." Suddenly it hit her. "Hey, why did you go back to work this morning anyway? You're right. It's not like you need the job, and you don't have to hide that you're not Mark anymore. Tessa is cool with it."

Jared pointed at the door briefly. "Chad would probably try to have me arrested for evil impersonation or something. Besides, there's only so many workers doing maintenance, and if I cut out, they're going to be swamped. I can handle another five days."

Warmth trickled through her. "You're one of the good guys, aren't you?"

"In spite of having money, you mean? Yeah, I guess. It's what I'd want others to do."

"My comment had nothing to do with you having money. I think I like you, Jared Gilliland."

He stopped in the middle of feeding the plumbing snake down the drain to turn his full-wattage smile on her. "I like you too, Keri Smith."

He stared for a minute, and she could feel his gaze on her lips, her body. Like a laser beam heating her up. "Stop that."

"Can't help it. If you mean the looking at you. You just..." He jerked his head away. "My wolf is not helping matters. We need a little time taking a run. When do we hit the next dry land?"

Even the mention of a run made something leap inside. "Ketchikan. We make port around seven tomorrow morning. We depart eight p.m."

"Then it's a date? I'm not on shift until afternoon. Can I

entice you to explore the island with me tomorrow morning?"

"Sounds wonderful."

She curled her arms around her legs and luxuriated in her happiness. Her wolf stopped making filthy suggestions of how to seduce her mate and instead preened in having chosen such a good match. *Yeah, yeah, you know everything.*

Her wolf agreed completely.

"You get the stolen stuff back to Tessa?"

She nodded then realized he couldn't see her as he'd turned his back to continue working. "First time I've seen her get snarly in a long time. She's very pissed off someone would dare to try to set up my mate for a fall."

"Well, people didn't know I was your mate, did they?"

"No, but she's still pissed." Keri had to smile. "It's funny. I started this trip wondering if I was going to have to hold Tessa's hand the entire time, but the more demands made on her the better she's stood up to the challenge."

"She's got the training, right? You said she graduated with honours?"

"Yeah. She's totally got the skills, only she's always comparing herself to her big brother who is like Mr. Perfection. That dude is freaky. It's not his fault that he's good at everything he does, but it..." She didn't want to seem disloyal to Tessa.

Jared dragged back hard on the snake, pulling something through the pipes. "It makes it tough for the people who follow behind? Yeah, I can see that. Especially in shifter families, it can get tough. Although cats are usually less into the 'I have bigger fangs than you'."

"Tony isn't competitive at all. He's this big old friendly pussycat, which is part of the reason I think he did such a good job coordinating. Everyone liked him, and they worked hard for him."

Jared tugged again, making a little more headway. "What's the story with Chad, then? He doesn't seem the type to be best buds with someone like Tony. Chad's the opposite of an overachiever."

Another tug. Another. Keri watched in fascination as he worked. "Nope. Makes perfect sense. Tony was too softhearted to fire Chad's ass. But to be honest, it sounds as if the way Chad's dealt with you this trip is the first time he's really stepped over the line. You know, acting like a shithead."

"Oh, I'm getting special treatment? How simply marvelous."

Keri snorted, the sound escalating into a cry of surprise as Jared gave one final tug and the stuck object burst into view.

An enormous, sodden stuffed polar bear with a ragged snout stared forlornly at them both as they laughed. Thievery and brother's evil friends completely forgotten in the moment of growing together.

Jared rested his muzzle along Keri's back, both of them still breathing hard from chasing each other through the tall timbers of the forest covering the mountains behind Ketchikan. They'd found a small open space overlooking the town, the highway between them and the brightly coloured square houses built in layers over the steep hillside.

"That was amazing. And just what I needed," Keri all but purred as she settled more comfortably.

Even speaking into her mind was more effort than he wanted to make. Lazy contentment poured through every one of his muscles, the morning sunshine bathing them with warmth. The harbour lay below them, not close enough for any more than the faint sound of human voices and wheels over the docks. Three massive ships stood in waiting, their passengers pouring through the small town like an invasion.

And every day that same invasion would repeat itself, but unlike the Vikings or Goths, these raids brought energy and finances to the people who lived and loved the remote land.

He would miss the North terribly if they left, and suddenly that had to be part of what he shared with her. *"Keri—we can live anywhere we want, you know that, right?"*

She quivered under him. *"I hear the words, but the pictures are not registering properly yet."*

"I understand. And I'm not pushing but need you to know I really love this kind of thing. The wilderness, and the small towns. The ability to shift and be completely wild within five minutes of leaving my house—if you've only experienced that kind of freedom while on a holiday, maybe you can't understand, but this is home for me."

She rolled belly up, and his wolf trembled to control the howl of delight that wanted to escape. Then she wiggled around and licked his muzzle, and he was even more floored.

"I have no home. No place that calls me to be there on holidays and special events. You are my mate, and while I want to have conversations about what's happening in our life, I'm too damn happy right now to try to figure out things I should complain about. I'm a wolf, Jared. I like dirt under my paws and the sun warming my fur. If you want to live in

the North, I'm good with it. If you want to take me to expensive places in Europe, I'll just have to grin and bear that."

She was all soft against him and he stared over the water contently. They watched the action for a good twenty minutes, Jared enjoying every one of the deep breaths he took that allowed more and more of her scent to fill his head.

"Too funny. Look."

Keri patted a paw toward the main street.

"Paws suck as fingers. What are you trying to show—wait a minute. Is that Chad sucking face with someone?"

Keri wiggled with her laughter. *"Oh wow, it's Eden from housekeeping. She's been all over his ass from what I heard. Chad was complaining about her to Tony between trips a while back, and Tessa mentioned it was happening this trip as well."*

Jared examined the near-to-sex-on-the-street happening up against the back wall of the side street. *"He doesn't seem to be complaining anymore."*

He was getting a little turned on. It had nothing to do with Chad—ick ick and triple ick—but everything to do with the fact he was picturing putting Keri into that same position up against the wall and doing a little enthusiastic sun-worshipping himself. *"Is your wolf happy? Shall we go grab a quick lunch?"*

Keri was on her feet and racing down the path to where they'd hidden their clothing. *"I say skip lunch and we can have sex until it's time for your shift."*

Even as they sprinted down the hillside, he couldn't believe his incredible good luck. He loved being a wolf. Loved having a mate.

And lunchtime trysts with his mate? Oh yeah...he was sure he was going to love those too.

essa wrinkled her nose as she accepted the handful of jewelry Keri passed over. "It just doesn't make any sense. I had a couple of the best noses on the ship go through all the crew quarters, and it's impossible to figure out from scent alone who's been stealing and hiding things. And when they were only hiding it on Jared, it was one thing. But now that it's spread to you?"

"That's why it's got to be a plant."

"It's driving me crazy how they've managed to stay one step ahead of me." Tessa offered another piece of chocolate.

Keri turned it down flat. "How the caffeine in that stuff doesn't make you crawl the walls, I'll never know."

"Who says it doesn't? I'm actually half-comatose normally."

Keri blew a raspberry then rose to her feet as Jared approached.

"May I interrupt?" He kissed her cheek, and Keri sighed like a lovelorn schoolgirl.

Tessa raised a brow. "You seem capable of doing

anything you put your mind to. Including mucking up my well-running cruise."

Jared shook his head slowly. "You're doing a great job. Everyone is giving glowing reports, the visitors and the staff, so relax and enjoy the final day."

Keri watched as Tessa visibly relaxed. "Really?"

"Of course. There's nothing but praise for the cruise, as usual. And the only mention I heard of anything weird with the jewelry were a few women I passed who were raving about the ship's 'cleaning service', whatever that is."

Tessa bounced. "Wheee! It worked."

"What you up to, girlie?" Keri asked, sneaking into Jared's arms for a quick hug.

"I had this brainwave to have the items cleaned before returning them, and made up these little cards 'complimentary sparkles to make your trip shine'... Well, the card said it better than that, but you get the idea. Like there was a reason for things to be slightly out of place. I guess it worked."

Keri snickered. "Only on a shifter ship, I bet. I wouldn't try that one on a human vessel. I think they'd be a little more suspicious."

"Totally." Tessa nodded. "Shifters are fun to work with —as long as nothing is gone for good, they're cool. I'm still upset I can't figure out who's taking things in the first place. We've got all kinds of shifters working the ship, so it's not as if I can get any of the Alphas on board to make demands until they find out who it is. Besides, that's the opposite side of what I want—this isn't a witch-hunt, and it's not supposed to be an inquisition either."

"If everything is in place by the end of the trip, and there are no outstanding complaints from passengers, is it even an issue anymore?" Keri really didn't want it to be an issue.

Tessa paused. "I can't just sweep it away, Keri." She stared up at both of them and shook her head. "I mean, I know you can't be the thieves, because, hello, you've been handing items over to me as fast as you find them, but it still looks bad. And if we can't point to the guilty party, there's bound to be someone who will suspect you, even afterward. Or suspect me of covering up your guilt."

It was too true. "Then we have to look faster. We have a few hours until we make dock. You don't need me for anything else?"

Tessa shook her head as she unwrapped another chocolate bar.

Jared waved a hand. "I'll help as well, but first, I wondered if you'd gotten any response to that message I sent to my pack."

The cat's grin grew again. "Oh yeah, there was one. Pretty brief, just that he'd meet you at the dock. Someone named Keil signed it."

A shudder shook her mate, and Keri squeezed him a little tighter. "Jared? You okay?"

He nodded. "Yeah, but I guess we'll be introducing you to my Alpha sooner than later."

"Oh."

"Don't worry, he's cool, only there's a long overdue discussion that needs to happen. Keil took over as Alpha after my folks left town, so he's not aware of a few things."

"Are you in trouble?"

"Hell, no. Just..." The buzzer on his waist belt went off and Jared sighed. He checked the screen and stepped away from Keri's side. "So much for helping you look around for the last few hours. Someone decided the shuffleboard lanes would be a great place to dump a couple of bottles of bubbles. There's no one available from housekeeping. I have to go clean it up."

He dropped a kiss on her cheek and turned.

"Wait—I'll go with you." She stepped in time with him as he pulled up next to a maintenance closet and opened the lock, dragging out a well-stocked cart. Mop and broom handles stuck out above the edge of the neat basket section. "I have no ideas other than sitting and staring at people anyway. I'm sorry, some troubleshooter I've been for us."

"It's going to be fine. Really."

Keri yanked her hair back and secured it with a ponytail holder. There was a light breeze again, this time pulling off the land, and with the ship's forward momentum, it was enough to make the flags on the railing snap and crackle, their bright colours adding a happy twist to the blues and greens of the surroundings.

The kids were having a blast in the bubbles. Not only kids—a couple of older cats had shifted to their animal forms to join in. They skidded across the surface, four paws splayed wide to the side for balance.

"That looks like a lot of fun." Jared put two fingers in his mouth and whistled, loudly. "Okay, everyone down to the right."

Keri frowned. "What are you doing?"

Jared grinned. "Well, I have to clean it up, but not this instant, and as long as they run from the railing toward the inner deck, they should be safe, right?"

Keri watched with admiration as Jared coaxed the gathering of a dozen or so youngsters into a safer starting position. More people gathered to watch the kids take a running start then swoosh across the solid wood boards that were now thoroughly coated with a thin layer of slick wet bubbles.

A cheer went up as Mr. Fedora joined the queue. He chatted with the youngsters around him as he waited for his turn.

"What's he up to?" Keri asked.

"A little fun? Just because he's an important person doesn't mean he can't have a good time with the simple things of life." Jared caught her hand in his, and they stood and enjoyed the sun shining down on them, the laughter and excitement in the air making her nearly able to forget there was a cloud hanging over them.

Fedora's form for the approach was superb, but his steady footing vanished at the three-quarter point of the run, much to the delight of the children who laughed and swooped in to help him to his feet.

"You going to try?" Jared asked her.

"Me? Nahhh." Only she eyed the deck and wondered if it was terrible that she wanted to join in.

He pushed her forward. "Go on. It's safe enough. Troubles will be there later, have some fun now."

She stood in the line, short people and adults all lined up for their own turn. One of the kids raced up to Jared with a couple of extra bottles of bubbles in his hands, and Jared leant over to discuss something—probably reloading the surface to make it slipperier. Just the way he turned his full attention on the child made Keri's heart ache. He had his hands planted on his thighs, his face turned wholly toward the little wolf as they discussed earnestly.

He was a good man, and Keri was falling in love. It wasn't enough her wolf was obsessed, she wanted her human mind to love her mate as well. And with every day that passed, she grew more confident love could happen.

Was happening.

Jared sent the child off with one bottle. The line of sliders paused as the little boy dribbled liquid from the open mouth of the bottle in a zigzag pattern over the length of the lane.

A slight commotion from the right drew her attention. Eden from housekeeping marched up to Jared then whispered loud enough that her voice, though not the specific words, could be heard from where Keri stood in the line.

Eden grabbed the railing of the cart and tugged it toward her. Jared laid a hand on the basket section and stopped her motion. That was when Keri spotted the neat *Eden* label on the upper edge of the basket and a horrible, terrible, yet wonderful thought hit her.

Jared gave up fighting, his hands lifted in the air, and Eden turned and flounced off, her cleaning cart in white-knuckle possession.

The little lad who was reloading the bubbles reached the end of the row and turned, giving a quick thumbs-up before racing back to Jared's side.

Keri rudely forced her way past the few shifters waiting in front of her. "Excuse me, sorry, emergency."

And with an extra burst of speed, she timed her leap to hit the lane first, her gaze locked on Eden as the woman scurried toward the maintenance-staff-only door, her cart clutched in front of her. Keri balanced as if on a skateboard, twirling in a full 360-degree circle as she fought to keep her balance. A loud roar of approval rose behind her. The wall of the inner cabin shot past her as she bore down on her target. They connected smartly, Eden's feet flying out from under her, and the cart tipping hard enough it landed with a bounce.

Mops flew one way, brooms and buckets another.

And over it all, a fine layer of earrings, necklaces and other shiny baubles came to rest on top of her and Eden.

12

He'd come full circle. Jared leaned back in the comfy couch, looking around the familiar coffee shop with something close to wonder rippling through him. Across the table, his Alpha lowered a tray filled with coffees and goodies. Jared still couldn't smell the damn stuff, but now it didn't matter in the least, because he had his mate at his side, her feet tucked under his thigh as she curled up tight against him.

"You two know how to make a splash." Keil dropped his bulk into a chair before passing a mug to Keri. "I thought I'd heard of everything, but this is..." He seemed to search for a proper word.

"Entertaining?" Jared supplied hopefully.

Keil snorted. "Better than having to haul your ass out of the slammer. You're a far more complicated guy than I ever imagined, Jared."

Across the table, Tessa leaned in and snagged a chocolate éclair, sinking her teeth into the soft surface and groaning happily. She swallowed quickly before pointing the half-eaten goodie at her best friend.

"You still need to explain what made you take out Eden like that."

Keri squirmed upward. "You know we'd talked about how maybe Chad was setting Jared up? But I couldn't figure out any reason for him to try to mess up the cruise. I mean, I knew he wanted your brother back in charge, but Tony isn't stupid, and while Chad isn't the brightest flashlight on the block, even he had to know ruining the ship's reputation wouldn't be the way to keep his friend happy."

Keil listened intently then wrinkled his nose. "So, there was no setup?"

Tessa licked her fingertips clean even as she shook her head. "There was a setup. Eden's been trying to get Chad's attention for the past three cruises, at least. My brother and I heard him talk about her, but he's always had someone else he was involved with."

"Including, he thought, Keri for the start of this trip," Jared teased.

"Well...yeah." His mate flushed nicely. Then her gaze narrowed. "You're one to talk, Mr. *Running away from my lover's brothers*. You gonna give me grief? Forget it."

Jared backpedaled. She had a point. "Go on, tell us the final bit."

Tessa shrugged. "Eden confessed. She knew if things went missing the two areas most likely to be accused of the thefts would be housekeeping or maintenance—the only groups with easy access to private quarters. She figured if she was sleeping with Chad, he'd be less likely to want to accuse her. After he'd complained about how much he disliked Jared, it was an easy step to drop some of her ill-gotten goods in a direction that made him look guilty. But, Keri, you slammed into her out of the blue. Spill...why?"

Keri snuggled against Jared's side. "Honest? There was

this art heist we learned about in school. The cleaning staff at one of the big museums were replacing priceless artwork with forgeries and rolling out the real art under the guards' noses unnoticed in their carts. When Eden got in such a snit over Jared grabbing her private cleaning cart, I wondered if there was something in there she didn't want found."

Tessa raised a brow. "So, like a total guess on your part is what you're saying."

Keri nodded. "Yeah, pretty much."

Tessa flashed her two thumbs up. "You rock as a troubleshooter."

Wild satisfaction rolled over Jared. Keri had saved their butts, because facts or not, it wouldn't have been easy to explain to his parents what had gone down on the ship.

They visited for a bit, everyone talking at the same time —easy conversation among people who honestly liked each other. Keri's hand rested in his, and he rubbed her fingers lightly, his mind racing as he considered what was the best thing for them to do next. They really did have a world of options open.

"Ahem."

Jared jerked to his feet. "Chad?"

The man's usual bluster was missing as he clutched his hat in his hands and avoided eye contact. He sighed wearily, then noticed Keil, his eyes widening before he dipped his head politely. "Sorry, didn't mean to interrupt. I'll give you a call—"

"Wait." Jared wasn't sure why, but he pulled the chair from the table behind them and offered it. "Sit. You want a coffee?"

Chad paused then joined them. He looked across to Tessa and let loose another one of those sighs. "No coffee, but I do owe you an apology, Tessa, and since I was rude in front of others, I should apologize in front of them. I had no idea Eden would do something so bizarre. I would never have jeopardized the cruise. I hope you believe me."

Tessa nodded slowly but didn't speak.

"You did a great job. I hope you enjoy running the ship for a long time to come." He rose to his feet and nodded, obviously ready to take his leave.

"Thank you for that," Tessa said. "Only I think I'm going to leave the ship to Tony from now on. I'll be sure to recommend he hire you on again."

Chad's jaw flapped open. "Really? I mean, *really?*"

Tessa shook a finger at him. "You're a great coordinator, Chad. You just need to lay off the private vendettas with crew members."

Chad glanced sheepishly at Jared. "Sorry about that."

Jared lifted his mug. "Totally forgotten."

Keri fidgeted at his side. "Tessa, you never said a word about not wanting to run the cruise ship next time out. What's up?"

"You were a little distracted." Tessa's wide grin was echoed in the expressions facing them.

Yeah, they'd been a trifle distracted, although who could blame them? Even sitting there Jared was aching to run off with Keri again, find somewhere private and not surface for days.

This mating thing—totally disruptive in more ways than he'd expected.

"Spill, girlfriend."

Tessa wiped chocolate from her lips. "I can't stand the ocean. I was borderline seasick the entire trip, and the only thing keeping me sane was the chocolate. If I don't want to be a three-hundred-pound cougar, I need to find a dry-land place to manage. The ship was fun, and I know I did a good job, but Tony is welcome to take the job back. I'm moving on to something that suits me better."

Keri laughed. "Now the chocolate makes sense. But... good for you. Yes, you need to do what's going to make you happy. I'm still proud of you."

Tessa smiled, and Jared relaxed.

If Tessa wasn't working the ship anymore, then perhaps Keri would be open to a little suggestion he had of his own.

He twisted her toward him and leaned their foreheads together. He spoke softly, just for her ears as the noise of happy voices rumbled around them. "Sad you don't have a job anymore?"

She shook her head. "I can't believe I'm unemployed—at least they didn't drop me off in Greenland."

He wasn't quite sure what that meant. "Does this mean you're free to do something special with me? Like maybe find a nice artsy job here in the North?"

"*I'm yours.*"

The words were simple, but there was lightness in her eyes, a kind of a joy and brightness heating up quickly to something that made his body catch fire. "*I'm glad to hear that.*"

He ignored everyone around them. Ignored the fact his Alpha was staring and had a ton of unanswered questions. Ignored everything but his need to connect with his mate, because right then there was nothing on his to-do list higher than "kiss Keri senseless".

So he did.

BONUS SCENE

New York City, three weeks later

Keri took a big breath and fought to keep her grin from getting even wider.

The past week had been like something out of a fairytale. She'd been whisked away by her mate to New York. Not just her, but her parents as well, and they'd attended all sorts of *meet the family* events. Including a wolfish ceremony that had been one step shy of a wedding, but more than formal enough to make her and her downhome, down-to-earth parents shake in their boots for a little while.

All that money. All that *power*—

Or at least they'd been nervous until they'd actually gotten together with Jared's family, at which point Keri had finally understood her mate's charm and good-nature must've been fifty percent genetics and fifty percent upbringing.

If there was a more relaxed, born-with-a-silver-spoon-in-their-mouths family, Keri couldn't imagine. Even now, at this very moment, her mother and father were off with the Gillilands, gallivanting somewhere through Central Park.

Or so Jared had just announced.

Keri glanced in the mirror to look over her shoulder at him a little more thoroughly, tempted to shake her head to see if what she'd heard rattled around in there. "Let me get this straight. My parents and your parents are strolling around Central Park. In their *wolf* forms."

Jared nodded. "It's a guarded group, of course, but my dad managed to set something up with bylaws and a tour company, so the only thing they have to be comfortable with is humans taking pictures of them, thinking they're *visiting wolf packs from Yellowstone.*" He grinned "You will not believe how much fun my dad has telling his shifter clients stories after spending a day in the park."

She returned to dragging a brush through her hair. The visit to New York was not at all what she'd expected. She was pleased to discover she was not only enjoying her mate's family, but most of all, her mate.

Inside, her wolf rumbled in agreement. *Like him. And wolf is sexy.*

Which was to the point, and true.

"So, if our moms and dads are currently gallivanting around a green space, what are we getting ready for?" She thought over the activities they'd enjoyed the past week. "Do your sisters want to take us somewhere? I like them, by the way. You have very nice sisters."

Jared folded his arms abruptly, but he looked far too content to be truly annoyed, even though his words came out teasingly. "Jilly and Julie most definitely want to spend more time with you, but I don't think I'm going to allow it. Not until I've found some ammunition to stop them from telling you more stories about my misspent youth. How am

I supposed to be your hero when you know I got stuck in a clown suit when I was twelve?"

Keri held up her hands. "Hey, don't look at me. You're the one who was precocious enough to shift that young. Also, *clown suit?* Don't you dare think about using that as a Halloween costume ever again."

A hint of mischief lit his eyes. "You don't like clowns?"

"No sane person likes clowns," she retorted. She rose to her feet and approached him threateningly.

Obviously not nearly as threateningly as she'd intended because the first thing he did when she came within reach was grab her by the lapels of her bathrobe and pull her in for a long, luscious kiss. One that had her toes curling and her body pounding like one big pulse.

Quite sometime later they separated, going in different directions by all of three inches, which was just enough room for her to catch her breath. "You keep doing that, and we're going to miss whatever it is we're supposed to attend."

"We can't have that, because we *are* the guests of honour." He reached behind him and pulled something from his back pocket. "Speaking of which, most notable guest of honour, this is for you."

Keri took the box from him, a slight hesitation before she spoke. "Jared, I know you're rich and all, but I love *you.* You don't need to keep buying me trinkets."

Trinkets that cost more than the rent on her apartment. The apartment she didn't need anymore because they'd gotten a place together. *Two* places, for heaven's sake. One in New York near his family, and one in Haines so they could officially stay with the Granite Lake pack.

He pressed a kiss to her cheek. "I love you too, but I'm not buying you trinkets because I'm worried about that. I'm giving you things because I just can't resist. But in this case, it's not my fault. This is a gift from the head of the *Scottish* wolf packs. Oh, and in a neat twist, this is also partly from one of the local families here in New York. Friends of my parents—their son and his best friend have something to do with the design, and I want to see what you think."

His comment intrigued her, and she lifted off the box lid, fully expecting to be blinded by the shimmer of diamonds or other precious jewels.

What she found instead was something a lot more rugged yet still equally beautiful. "Oh, *my*. This is amazing."

She pulled the unique item from the box and laid it in her palm, running her fingers over the braided cord that formed the bulk of the bracelet. Thin strands of copper wove through the cord, creating a mosaic of subtle beauty while still somehow being soft as silk.

Jared pulled it gently from her fingers and wrapped it around her wrist, doing up the clasp. "I take it that's approval?"

Keri stretched out her arm and twisted her wrist to allow the light to bounce off the thin strands of copper. "I do love the jewelry your family makes, but this looks functional as well as pretty." She glanced up at him. "Does it have more than one use?"

He shook her finger at her as he was grinning. "I knew you would catch on quickly. Yes. It's a line of jewelry suitable for shifters to wear in the wilderness. Not only does it have the same funky magic that the jewelry my family makes has, so it adjusts in size when you shift, all the items in this line can be unraveled. The bracelet gives you enough high test cord to create a lean-to."

"And the copper? Are we installing electricity in teeny little houses for creatures in the wilderness?"

"We could if we wanted to," he teased, reaching past her onto the dresser for a box she hadn't noticed. "And this one, if you can believe it, unravels into a hammock."

She pulled the lid off the second box far more eagerly, sucking in a breath at the beautiful necklace revealed. This time the copper radiated into a flaring sun, the cording braided far more intricately, but still skin-tantalizingly soft. "It would be a crime to destroy something this beautiful, because I would never be able to re-weave it."

"Here's the kicker. If you ever decide to use it, all you do after is return the cording to a central mailbox for recycling, and they'll send you a brand-new one."

"That is incredible, and makes absolutely no sense." She lifted her hair away from her neck so he could drape the necklace in place and fasten it. "How could that possibly be financially viable?"

Jared seemed a little distracted, pressing his lips against her neck and lingering there, teasing with his lips and tongue. "The fellow investing in the production line thinks the high initial cost means it's worthwhile, and hey, who am I to argue with a fellow billionaire about how he spends his money?"

Keri twisted in Jared's arms, playing her fingertips over his shoulders. "I had no idea wolf billionaires were a diamond a dozen here in New York, or I would have made a trip far sooner."

"Jim's a *bear* billionaire," Jared corrected her. "And you know, it really doesn't matter how many billionaires there are walking the streets—you've already got the only one you need."

She slid in against him, natural as breathing, pressing their lips together and answering his comment in a very thorough and enjoyable manner.

Before she knew it, one thing led to another, which meant they *were* a little late out to the gathering. Keri was a little more rumpled than she'd planned on, but pacing at Jared's side with her fingers linked in his, she wasn't about to worry.

Guests of honour were allowed to look rumpled.

His sisters waved from the opposite side of the garden area, jumping up and down to get her attention.

"I don't suppose I can convince you to behave this time," Jared mumbled as they came closer to where two young ladies stood visiting with a distinguished-looking elderly gentleman.

"I promise I will be as demure and quiet as anyone in your family."

His snort of amusement was enough to let her know *he knew* exactly what she'd just said.

THEY WERE INSTANTLY SURROUNDED, the senior shifter holding out his hand to Keri first, clasping her hand and lifting it so he could press a kiss to her knuckles. "And there they be. 'Tis a good thing for an old man's heart to see two young pups so in love."

Jared offered an introduction. "Keri, I'd like you to meet Sir William McGregor, of the McGregor clan of Scotland. He's the one who gave you the gifts today. Sir William, my mate, Keri Gilliland. Or soon to be Gilliland."

It was definitely a sign she'd been breathing rarefied air all week, because other than the quick shot thrilling through her, she managed to smile and dip her head politely instead of falling over in a faint. "The gifts are marvelous, and thank you. But I think meeting you is even more exciting."

The old man's eyes sparkled. He turned to her mate and

laid a firm hand on his shoulder. "Jared, lad. Are ye *sure* I can't convince ye to move to Scotland? I'd dearly love to pass on the clan to a wolf as brilliant as ye must be, selecting a mate as charming and glorious as this lassie."

Jared laughed as he tucked his arm further around Keri's waist, securing her to his side. "Thank you for the compliment, but you'll have to find some other equally brilliant wolf. We have plans in North America."

The gentleman dipped his head, then turned with a mischievous smile to Keri. "Of course. But you can come visit me anytime you'd like, me darlin' lass."

Jared laughed. "My parents warned me you could just about charm the birds from the trees, but you can't charm my mate away from me."

"He's welcome to try, though," Keri teased. "I do appreciate charming scoundrels. Obviously."

Laughter ensued, then they moved on, joining in the games of the evening, which of all things involved lawn bowling. Keri gossiped with Jared's sisters, admired dresses and jewelry, and listened to tall tales from Sir William and other elderly guests. Jared stayed by her side the entire time, and she felt herself falling more and more in love with this generous man who did his best to keep her smiling all the time.

It was dark by the time they slipped inside their suite, the dancing lights of the city sparkling outside the penthouse window. Keri ignored everything else and went straight to her mate, wrapping herself around him and pressing her hands to his cheeks to give him a long, slow kiss.

A kiss full of gratitude, and happiness, and all of the wonderful, bubbling-up, joyful emotions that had been filling her ever since she'd truly known he was hers.

Jared rested his hands on her hips and held her close, kissing her back, then nuzzling her with affection when their lips finally parted. "Well now, I don't know what brought that on, but I like it."

"You're not what I expected," she admitted. "And that's not your fault, it's mine for not having a good enough grasp of reality. The money wrapped around you is like wallpaper. Shiny and pretty, but it wouldn't look nearly so nice if it wasn't being placed on something solid and straight in the first place." She tipped his chin down again so she could kiss him once more. "I'm very glad my mate is such a wonderful man."

"And I'm glad my mate is you—"

They didn't need any words after that. They had a whole different language to speak in, for a very long time.

EPILOGUE

Mark Weaver had a good enough sense of humour to see the irony of the situation.

He leaned against the wall of the pack house and stared into the gathering of wolves, all of whom were making an excessive amount of noise, even by shifter standards. Which was saying a lot, considering wolves usually operated at maximum volume in the first place.

His gaze lingered for a moment on the corner of the room where the older members of the pack had stubbornly held onto a set of tables and chairs so they could ignore the music and dancing chaos around them and enjoy a game of cards. That they could focus in the middle of the ruckus said a lot about their concentration, or perhaps more about how much their hearing had deteriorated, but Mark wasn't about to judge.

They were having a good time, and that's what counted.

If only it could be said for him. The *having a good time* part.

He took another sweeping glance through the dancing

and laughing pack as he double-checked inside for a green-eyed monster.

Ah, there it was, just as he'd expected. Tucked not too far away, gloomy and morose.

His wolf huffed at his imagination. *Not gloomy. Also, not a dragon.*

I wasn't talking about you, Mark informed him. *It's an...expression.*

Another huff, this one more long-suffering as his inner wolfie settled into a state of calm acceptance. *Silly human. I'm the only wild beast in here.*

If Mark was honest, his wolf was right—there *was* a hint of jealousy bubbling inside, but it wasn't a malicious, snarling, clawing beast. More like his dragon of discontent had settled on its haunches and now sat in a slouched heap, shoulders drooped in a pout, head hanging low. All the fire in its belly extinguished.

Yes, that was Mark's version of being a jealous fool. More like an *I wish I had that. Why can't I have that?* whine as he commiserated with his inner green beastie.

His wolf offered a reassuring pat even as it repeated the earlier comment. *Silly human. We will find a mate someday, but in the meantime, we're doing the right thing.*

The kicker of it was Mark knew that. Which was why, as the guest stars of the evening marched toward him, the smile he forced to his face was nearly sincere. "Congrats again, and welcome to the pack, Keri."

He thought about putting his arms around the dark-haired brunette now standing in front of him and giving her a quick hug, just to jerk Jared's chain, but with them being newly mated and all, Mark might end up pulling back two bleeding stumps before he got a chance to explain he wasn't really poaching or doing anything uncool.

He held out his hand instead.

Keri smiled sweetly as she shook it. "Thanks. And you are?"

Jared wrapped an arm around her shoulders and tugged her against his side a little proprietarily and a whole lot *gloatingly*. "This marvelous fellow is the source of all our blessings. The bountiful matchmaker to our mating."

Mark somehow managed to keep from rolling his eyes, impressed when Keri managed to figure out Jared's non-information information, her eyes widening. "You're Mark."

"The one and only."

"Well, not really the *one and only*," Jared teased, "Because you know, there *were* two of you at the same time if we want to be technical about—" Keri shoved her elbow into his ribs, and Jared stopped, but his enormous grin remained.

Mark ignored everything else and focused on what was most important. "I hope you guys are wickedly happy together. And whenever you're in Haines, let me know if I can ever do anything for you."

Even as he said it, serenity slipped over him like a calming balm. *This* was who he was. Laid-back, relaxed.

Long-suffering...

For once Jared didn't take advantage and keep pushing, which Mark really appreciated. It was bad enough he'd missed the opportunity to work on the cruise ship for a couple of weeks, there were all sorts of other things that had gone wrong during the time Jared and Keri had taken off for a bit of a wolfie honeymoon.

Keri's expression turned inquisitive. "I do thank you for the meet and greet your absence unknowingly created, but I admit, I'm curious. Why did you not show up for work that day?"

Once again Mark found himself between a rock and a hard place. What he really wanted to do was admit the truth, which would then put him into a far better light in the eyes of a beautiful woman. Because even if she and Jared were mated, it was never a bad thing to have a woman talk about you as if you were one of the good guys.

But admitting the truth would mean throwing someone he cared about under the bus, someone innocent who deserved to be protected. That was something Mark could not, and would not, do. Which meant he had to revert to his usual.

Lock his smile in place and proceed to say nothing about his real reasons. Not really a lie, but not the truth, which meant he was going to look like an idiot. "Something came up, and I just couldn't make it. But hey, one man's disaster is another man's treasure."

Jared and Keri grinned at each other, their smiles exceedingly bright and out of line for how poor his joke had been.

She nodded, he punched Mark good-naturedly in the shoulder, then they were off to the next group for good wishes.

Mark watched them walk away. The dragon of jealousy put his head down on the ground and let out a long, steamy snort, all the fire inside dying with a final wimpy stream of half-hearted smoke and ash.

This was his life for now, and that was it. Mates and adventures would have to wait while he took care of the most important thing he had left.

But someday adventure would come calling.

He was sure of it.

~

New York Times Bestselling Author Vivian Arend
brings you a series of light-hearted,
stand-alone novellas, with fated mates and always a
happily-ever-after.

~

Granite Lake Wolves
Wolf Signs
Wolf Flight
Wolf Games
Wolf Tracks
Wolf Line
Wolf Nip

~

ABOUT THE AUTHOR

New York Times and *USA Today* bestselling author Vivian Arend loves to share the products of her over-active imagination with her readers. She writes contemporary, western, and light-hearted paranormal romances. The stories are humorous yet emotional, usually with a large cast of family or friends, and a guaranteed happily-ever-after.

Vivian lives in British Columbia, Canada, with her husband of many years—her inspiration for every hero and a willing companion for all sorts of adventures.

Find out more at www.vivianarend.com.

www.ingramcontent.com/pod-product-compliance
Lightning Source LLC
Chambersburg PA
CBHW031002210726
48290CB00007B/2432